Praise for Ellen's Song in the Finnish press

"Ellen's Song is a literary pearl. ...Ben Kalland tells a masterful tale about family secrets and impossible choices."

– Anna (women's magazine)

"It's difficult to explain the beauty of the moments in the book. Some of them I found myself contemplating weeks after reading. As if I had been there myself, in the middle of everything."

– Kodin Kuvalehti (general interest magazine)

"Kalland's writing is fresh. ...It piques your interest like a camera when it zooms into a surprising detail. A brilliant, balanced, and satisfying story both on an intellectual and an emotional level."

– Kulttuuri kukoistaa (book blog)

"Kalland writes gracefully and awakens the reader's interest by gradual revelation of the past. Some secrets are just hinted at, and readers need to be alert."

– Kouvolan Sanomat (newspaper)

"One of the most interesting novels this year. Ben Kalland starts his novel with the perfect sentence, one that forces the reader to devour the book. ...The novel presents a dysfunctional family where happiness is less important than keeping up appearances."

– Kauppalehti (economic journal)

"Ellen's passion for music is rendered with immense beauty."

– Etelä-Suomen Sanomat (newspaper)

"The past opens up to the reader: family secrets in Finland and the USA, the Jehovah's Witnesses organization in the background. ...The twists are surprising. ...A melancholy piece of writing, complete and beautiful."

– Hämeen Sanomat (newspaper)

"The description of the summers in the archipelago and the portrait of the young violinist, Ellen, are beautiful."

– Pohjalainen (newspaper)

"It's always interesting to get a peek into a close-knit organization that few outsiders have real knowledge about. ...What part of the tragedy is because of the religion? What influences our lives? How and when? Kalland leaves that to the reader. This is one of the strongest points of this novel."

– Helsingin Sanomat (newspaper)

"The multilayered story is revealed one piece at a time. The narrator, Markus Douglas, is a leader within the Jehovah's Witnesses. There are not many novels describing the organization this close and personal. The author describes the hierarchical practices of the organization, the struggle for power and the controlling of people's lives."

– Sana (Christian newspaper)

Ellen's Song

Ben Kalland

FENDERI

Published by Fenderi

First published in hardback by Atena in 2017

Original title in Finnish: *Vien sinut kotiin*

English editing by Mary Harris

Graphic design by Anna Makkonen

Copyright © 2018 Ben Kalland

23.1.20.09

ISBN 978-952-94-0193-2 (printed)

ISBN 978-952-94-0194-9 (Mobi)

Part I

Ellen

BEN KALLAND

1

On the same day I was about to travel from New York to Helsinki to attend Sofia's funeral, I got a letter from an unknown woman. She claimed to be my daughter.

I was on my way to meet Ron Miller when the receptionist in the lobby of our headquarters handed me an envelope. At first, I thought it was some kind of an internal notification. The envelope was white and neutral, and it looked like the envelopes my employer would use, but there was no logo on it. My name was written by hand in thin handwriting, and the address was correct, but there was an unnecessary addition, Brooklyn, which was underlined three times.

This was the first time in ten years I had received a real handwritten letter. Normally I got only bills or electronic mail. But I was in a hurry, so I had no time to open the envelope. I just stuffed it into my pocket.

Ron Miller seemed annoyed when I told him that I had to travel to Finland.

"Don't get me wrong," he said, "but this is ill-timed. You were supposed to ensure the outcome of the voting."

When somebody says "*don't get me wrong*," there is usually no risk of getting it wrong. I knew what Miller meant by ill-timed. In a few days, the board was supposed to vote, and the outcome was uncertain. I didn't like the prospect of having to leave the country in the middle of everything, but I had no choice.

"It may be difficult for me to influence the voting when I'm abroad."

"Markus," he said. "If you think it's important, you'll find a way. If you don't think it's important, you'll find an excuse."

I knew how to handle him. I chose my words prudently as if I was stepping on slippery stones and deliberated where to put my foot.

"It's not my fault that Sofia died." I was careful to make it sound like a statement, not like an accusation.

Miller seemed stupefied. There was a death in my family, and now I offered him the role of the insensitive boss. He immediately backed off. He wasn't as coldhearted as he sometimes seemed to be.

"I apologize, Markus," he said. "Of course not. I'm sorry for your loss. No hurry, we'll make the decision later. Of course you may go home."

Miller was my boss and my friend. Not the kind of friend you call in an emergency, but the kind of friend who has the same goals you do. I had worked for Miller for years, and usually we got along. But lately something had changed. There had been an almost imperceptible shift in our relationship, like continental drift or like when a child grows, something you realize only after the fact.

I got the rest of the week off. I took my compact weekend bag, packed with precision, and bought a paperback at the airport. Before I boarded the plane, I texted Carola, telling her my flight number. She immediately replied that she already was in Helsinki taking care of some practical matters with Sofia's husband.

The gate closed, and we rolled onto the tarmac.

Instructions on how to use lifejackets and oxygen masks. All electronic devices in flight mode, luggage under the seat in front of you.

Only when we were flying over the ocean, when I had had dinner with my elbows squeezed together and my knees against the seat in front of me and the man sitting next to me had fallen asleep, did I remember the letter.

It was short, only a few lines.

"Dear Markus Douglas, We have never met, but I am your daughter. I have grown up without a father, but since I now have a daughter myself, I want her to learn to know you. I suggest we meet at the corner of Flatbush Avenue and Plaza Street, Tuesday April 19th, at 1 pm."

The signature was written in the same thin handwriting: *Ellen Leblanc.* There was a telephone number, no address.

Now, in retrospect, it's easy to see that there were many clear signs that I missed. If I had looked at the map to see where the corner of Flatbush and Plaza was, I might have suspected something. But now I just wondered why the woman wanted to meet on a street corner.

I didn't recognize the name, though I should have. Leblanc sounded French Canadian. If the woman had a small child, she probably was twenty or thirty herself, give or take a few years. I counted backward in time and tried to find a connection to Montreal or Toronto or Canada at least, some reason why somebody would say something so outrageous. That's why I didn't catch the most obvious clue, her first name.

Ellen.

My kid sister was called Ellen. She was three years younger than Carola and I were, and she was the musician in the family. As a child, she played soloist for symphony orchestras, and once she caused a sensation when she played a borrowed Stradivarius at a student concert. When she was fifteen, she participated in the International Jean Sibelius Violin Competition.

I have had a number of relatives called Ellen; it's a recurring name. In every generation, there has been at least one Ellen. My grandmother was Ellen. My aunt, the black sheep of the family we never talk about, was called Helena, a name that has the same roots.

Now somebody called Ellen claimed to be my daughter.

There was no stamp as the letter had been delivered in person. I examined the envelope as if it could tell me something, and when I turned it over, a photograph fell to the floor. I had to unlatch my seat belt to retrieve it. I expected the photo to show a twenty-something woman whose features supposedly proved that we were related, or perhaps my alleged grandchild. But there was no woman or child in the picture.

It was a picture of me.

When you tell a story, you can choose your point of view and what you want to include in the story. You can choose in many ways, and by choosing carefully, you can shape the story any way you like.

This story is about Ellen.

I choose to include moments that now feel important. They are fragments of the whole, small pieces of the puzzle. They are only memories, but they are slices of reality.

I will start with a cold January night in Porkkala, in southern Finland.

That night, when we were standing on the ice, when all the colors were transformed into monochrome aluminum and brushed steel, and the coldness felt like the whole universe was holding its breath, that night is not the chronological start of this story. But it is the point where everything comes together, everything that happened before and everything that happened after.

2

It has now been dozens of years since the accident, but many people who live in Porkkala still remember it. Now, years later, it's impossible to tell who was to blame. Perhaps we all were to some extent because there were so many things that shaped the outcome. Our habit of managing all internal conflicts ourselves. The coldness, the ice, too much wine and beer. Unnecessary risk-taking.

Our summer cottage, Bellevue, was at the sea, about three-quarters of a mile from the road leading to the pilot station. We didn't visit Bellevue that often during wintertime because the last stretch of road was narrow and the snow was never plowed. But that winter was practically snowless, the earth was frozen, and you could drive almost to the end of the road.

It was a Saturday at the end of January. It wasn't that cold earlier in the day, just a couple of degrees below freezing. The sky was overcast but toward the evening, the sky cleared up, and when the sun set, the stars were brighter than ever. There were a dozen of us, boys and girls, most of us in our late teens. Some of the others took bus number 607 from Kirkkonummi, some got a lift with Timo Auramo. Carola and I had arrived earlier to heat the cottage.

The cottage was ours, but Timo Auramo took the lead, assuming the role of the supervisor. Everybody brought their share of food and drinks: barbecue meat, sausages, bread, wine, and beer. Something sweet for dessert. Timo organized the bar-becue, arranged the construction of a long dinner table, and he lit the fire in the sauna. He was the oldest, but many of us were annoyed by him playing the lead, taking his liberties, especially with the girls. He flirted with everyone and was particularly interested in Carola, but my sister wasn't interested at all and asked me not to leave her alone with him. I myself had a crush on Paula.

There are many versions of what happened that night, and most of them tell the same story until midnight. The meal passed as expected and after we had had a few glasses of wine, the mood became increasingly cheerful.

Timo had made sure that the fire in the sauna was lit at all times. Because the sauna was big, however, it didn't warm up until ten. Initially, we had planned for the girls to go in the sauna first, but since it took such a long time for the sauna to warm up, we decided to go all at the same time. Some of us may not have wanted to—Paula at least was a bit shy—but we had had wine and beer, and when we made the decision to go mixed, it would have required more courage to refuse than to simply go along.

We were all sitting on the sauna bench, and the hot air from the stove hit our faces. A quick poll revealed that Carola and I were the only ones who had ever swum in the freezing water in a hole in the ice. The decision was made: this night all of us would skinny-dip in the icy water.

Both ice holes had a thin layer of ice on them. We used an iron bar and a piece of wood to break the ice of the hole that was closer to the jetty. We put an oil lamp on the ice to light it.

One at a time, we dipped ourselves into the water. Paula was one of the first. She walked to the hole wrapped in a towel, looked into my eyes, let the towel fall. The lamp illuminated her body for a moment. *I'm not afraid*, her eyes told me. Then she put her hands on the edge of the ice to support herself and slid into the water.

We helped her back onto the ice and gave her a round of applause. After that, nobody could refuse to do it. One after another, we all slid into the black water.

Later, when we were sitting in the warmth of the sauna again, everybody remarked how the skin felt tight and the blood flowed faster and how the water strangely felt warmer than the air. But I think most of us thought it was a rather scary experience, not a refreshing one.

We went back to the cottage to spend the rest of the evening. Around midnight, most of us turned in. Some had had too much to drink and had passed out. That's why they had nothing to tell afterward and nobody questioned our story.

During the night the temperature fell considerably. At two in the morning, it was - 18°.

The four of us who were still awake decided to go to the sauna again. Paula and I, Timo and Carola. Timo was the one who suggested the sauna, but it's unclear whose idea it was to open the other ice hole too. It's possible that it was my or Carola's idea, but I think it was Timo's. He wanted to show off and impress the girls. Perhaps he thought no one of us would dare.

Carola and I had tried swimming under the ice a couple of times before, but only in broad daylight. The distance between the holes was ten yards, and if you swam a couple of strokes and kicked with your foot on the underside of the ice, it took only a moment to swim from one hole to the other. But in complete darkness, ten yards is a long way. Even though we were tired and slightly drunk, we weren't stupid. We understood that an oil lamp wouldn't be enough. Timo fetched a torch from his car.

We warmed up in the sauna. I think Timo was a bit scared. I was.

I wanted to impress Paula, so I decided to go first. Carola put the oil lamp at the second hole and Timo illuminated the ice between the holes with his torch.

The water was black. I was barefoot but didn't feel the cold. I was so focused on the task that I felt nothing. I left the towel on the edge of the ice and slid into the water and immediately submerged my head. If you hesitate, you will panic, and it will be impossible to force yourself into the darkness.

I lost my bearings. In daylight, the underside of the ice gleams, and you can see the other hole. But in the dark, you lose your internal compass, and the cold water presses against your temples and the invisible ice scratches your skin.

The ice was four inches thick. Thick enough to bear the weight of a person, thin enough to allow Timo's torch to shine through the ice crystals like a pale January sun. I swam a couple of strokes toward the hazy light. I didn't feel the cold; I focused my whole consciousness on the light. I was alone. I wasn't far away from the others, but there was a boundary, I was in my own strange world.

I wasn't really terrified at that particular point in time. I realized that I could just stop, let the air out of my lungs, and slowly sink into the darkness down below. I could have chosen the silence and the darkness, but I headed for the light. It moved forward, and I knew that I couldn't turn back. I followed the light, held my breath, swam one more stroke, and then my head was above the surface, and the light exploded into my eyes.

I have read that you can get addicted to the rush of adrenaline, and I think I understand mountaineers and other athletes who expose themselves to risks. You lose your sense of time, your field of vision narrows down, you are absorbed. Later, you may think that you are unbreakable.

Timo and Carola helped me up again. I had spent only seconds under the surface, but it felt like an eternity. I was euphoric. I had survived.

We warmed up in the sauna again. We didn't talk. I had done it, now it was their turn.

Paula wanted to go next. With a little help from the wine, she had gotten rid of her shyness and her fear. When her head disappeared under the surface, we steered her toward the other hole by lighting the ice a couple of feet in front of her. You couldn't distinguish her naked body, it was just a formless shape under the snow-free ice, as if seen through a shower curtain or sand-blasted glass.

When her head reappeared in the other hole, I realized that I had been holding my breath. I exhaled at the same time she did.

When Timo dived under the ice, I held the torch. Or maybe Carola held it. I'm not sure. When I think about that moment, I see it through a lens that distorts and crops, my memory. I can see outlines and shadows, but the details are gone.

I don't have an explanation for what happened. Today I can't remember or even imagine the emotions that guided us. Sometimes we make decisions that cement our fate for all eternity. We can later study these decisions from all angles, like you study a fly caught in amber, but we can never undo them.

Maybe Timo was a bit too confident, a bit too arrogant, maybe he had taken too many liberties. Maybe we wanted to teach him a lesson, make him more humble.

Sometimes I think that we made a joint decision to scare him. Sometimes I'm sure it all happened by accident.

We guided him in the wrong direction, toward the open sea.

Timo was strong. He swam a couple of strokes toward the light, and we moved it farther, in the direction of Stenskär Island and Madame Island and the lighthouse, and suddenly Timo had swum ten yards in the wrong direction. We moved the light even farther. Timo followed.

We looked at each other and at the black horizon. We said nothing but we made a silent decision: just a few more yards toward the sea. Paula said something; she thought we were going too far.

Then we had had enough. Timo had learned his lesson, it was time to wrap up. We moved the torch in the right direction, toward the other hole.

But how do you communicate through four inches of ice that it was a joke, that the right direction is ninety degrees to the left?

Timo stopped. He hesitated. He swam one more stroke toward the horizon. We stamped on the ice, swung the torch, and finally he got it and turned around.

At that very moment, Carola dropped the torch. No, at that moment I dropped the torch. Carola tripped and dropped the torch, and the lid opened, and the batteries fell to the ground. Or maybe I tripped, managed to keep the torch in my hand, but accidentally turned it off. Paula said that the torch went off by itself. She couldn't remember who held it.

At the time, the phrase "light pollution" was not yet commonly used, but in the city, there were lights everywhere. Neon signs, streetlights, shop windows. Even in the middle of the night, there was always some light. But here, far away at the sea, the darkness was black.

When the light went off, we didn't see anything at all, because our eyes had adapted to the sparkling light of the torch. If we had looked, after a while maybe we would have been able to see the stars. It could have been a beautiful moment, serene. The coldness, the ice, all the familiar constellations, more detailed than ever, a million stars you can only see when the sky is free from clouds and it's nearly twenty degrees below zero.

Carola shook the torch, removed the batteries and put them back in. I tried too. My fingers were stiff from the cold. I tried to feel with my fingers which way the batteries should be inserted. I didn't feel anything. I dropped the towel.

The only things we could see were the stars and the faint light from the sauna window.

Paula cried.

When we finally got the torch working, Timo was straight under us, face up. We couldn't see his eyes, just a bizarre shape, his nose flat against the ice. He tried to break the ice from below, but his movements were sluggish and powerless.

We moved the light, hoping he would swim in the right direction. We yelled at him and at each other. Paula was hysterical. We shook with cold, but there was no time to worry about that. We tried to break the ice by jumping up and down and then we used the iron bar. When Timo stopped moving, I jumped into the water and Carola guided me toward him but he was already sinking and he was too heavy and I didn't have any air left and I thought I would drown.

When the police and the diver arrived, both ice holes were frozen again.

I was eighteen in the picture the unknown woman had sent me. It had been taken at Bellevue, during late summer apparently, about six months before the accident. In the background, you could see the sauna, a bit of the open sea toward the Porkkala fjard, and Madame Island. The sunlight was glittering on the water. I was smiling. The picture was like the final recorded evidence of our summer paradise, taken a moment before it was gone.

Carola was interested in photography, and the picture was probably taken with her camera. But the horizon was tilted, and the composition was sloppy, so I assumed that one of my younger sisters, Sofia or Ellen, had taken it.

That summer was our last summer at Bellevue. We didn't spend that much time in Porkkala during that summer because I had a job at a print shop and Carola worked at a department store and Ellen rehearsed for the Sibelius Violin Competition together with her accompanist. Sofia and our parents probably spent a bit more time at the cottage.

We took care of each other then. We were a family, and nobody could tear us apart.

Within a year after the picture was taken, our lives had changed for good. Our family was split, and we had stopped talking to each other.

3

When the taxi arrived at the Hietaniemi chapel, it was almost one-thirty in the afternoon. I looked over the groups of people in black clothes and searched for familiar faces. Some of them I recognized even though it had been years since we met, and I shook their hands. Others I just nodded at, enough to acknowledge them, but not enough to invite a strained conversation.

Sofia's sons and her husband were standing together, close to the entrance. My father was standing alone. He wasn't as straight-backed as he used to be, he was in his eighties, eighty-two or eighty-three. I remembered the year of his birth but not his birthday.

Carola was standing a bit farther away. She removed her sunglasses, and our eyes met for a second. I nodded almost indiscernibly, clearly enough that she could see it, but not so much that anybody else noticed. We were staying in the same hotel and had planned to meet afterward.

I checked the time on my mobile phone. I had intended to visit the family grave before the funeral, but there was no time for that. The urn with Sofia's ashes would be lowered into the grave after the cremation, but the ceremony would take place the following week, and by that time I would already be back in New York.

The funeral guests started drifting toward the entrance. A couple of young women, who apparently didn't know who

Carola was, greeted her politely, wearing the pious and solemn demeanor of funeral guests who are not among the closest bereaved. Others avoided her, turning their heads away.

Carola sat down in the same row of chairs as I, but she thoughtfully left a few empty seats in between us. A young man, who looked like someone who liked to be in charge, touched her shoulder.

"These seats are reserved for close relatives, but you may sit over there."

She looked him in the eyes.

"I'm Sofia's sister," she said. "I prefer to sit here."

The man opened, then closed his mouth, like a little boy who had rehearsed for a school play and had forgotten his most important line or gotten an answer that wasn't in the script. I raised my hand to let him know that I had the situation under control. My father pretended not to notice; he just stared at Sofia's white coffin.

The funeral proceeded as usual, the talk only briefly touching Sofia's life and death. Mostly it was about the hope of resurrection and eternal life.

I wondered why Carola was even there, why she had flown in from Paris to attend a half-hour ceremony with meaningless speeches. Just to say goodbye to a sister she hadn't been talking to for years?

I, of course, had no choice, I had to be there, but the truth was that Sofia wasn't the closest one of my three sisters. When we were children, Carola, Ellen, and I were always together. Sofia was too little to tag along. Last time I met her was more than ten years ago when I previously visited Finland. It had ended in embarrassment: I happened to witness a conjugal fight between Sofia and her husband, Arto. If anything, I wanted to avoid getting dragged into other people's domestic arguments.

I couldn't even remember exactly what Sofia looked like. Instead, I remembered photographs from our childhood. A two-year-old Sofia, sitting on the floor of our cottage, her diapers wet, crying because Mother was sleeping all the time. Five-year-old Sofia, watercolors on her face, "I'm an Indian." Ten-year-old Sofia in front of the mirror, Ellen combing her hair. Soon she lost that innocent look; she stopped talking to Carola when she was twelve. She became a sweet but not beautiful teen. She married young, to a wastrel ten years her senior and got three sons but not the daughter she wished for. She never left the country, and she died in a stupid accident, drowning in six inches of water at the jetty at her summer cottage.

There was a funeral reception at restaurant Perho, but of course, Carola wasn't invited.

After the reception, I had to work in my hotel room. It was morning in New York, and I had emails to write and phone calls to make. Ron Miller had decided not to postpone the voting after all, so I had to do my best working remotely. Even though I didn't have the right to vote myself, I felt uncomfortable not being there. If anything, my years in New York had taught me that if you want to influence something, you'd better be present.

4

We had to use the GPS device to find our way out of the city because there were too many one-way streets. When we approached Kirkkonummi County, I had trouble finding the right byroad. Road 51 had been rebuilt; there were unfamiliar exits and signs. When I saw the sign to Porkkala and we took the exit, the sexy voice inside the GPS suggested that I make a U-turn whenever possible.

A few miles later, I started recognizing the surroundings and the navigator settled down and predicted that we would arrive at our destination in twenty minutes.

It had been nearly forty years since last time we visited our cottage, Bellevue. The road toward the sea had been straightened out, but it was easy to recognize the familiar houses.

We had traveled this road hundreds of times during our childhood. I could see myself sitting in the front seat of bus number 607, Carola and Ellen sitting on the other side of the aisle. Ellen is hugging her violin, and she's humming. It's just the three of us. Mother is already at Bellevue together with Sofia, and Father is working. He has put us on the bus by ourselves. Probably this didn't happen that many times, but this is how I remembered it.

I parked the car at the turnaround. The mailbox still had Sofia and Arto's last name on it, in tilted golden letters. Carola removed the stickers with her fingernail.

The wooden stairs down to the sea were renewed. The old stone jetty had been removed and replaced by a pontoon. There was a buoy, but no boat. The path from the cottage to the sauna had been covered with slate.

We took the stairs down.

"One hundred," I said.

"Ninety-nine," Carola said.

This was something we used to quibble about as children. Were you supposed to count the last step or not, the one that was level with the ground?

Inside the cottage, it looked like everything of value had been collected and evacuated in a rush, as if the inhabitants had been expecting an invasion. There were light patches on the walls where the paintings had been. A pile of dirty clothes on the floor. The remaining furniture was broken. This was expected, and I was relieved that we didn't have to make decisions about what to keep. Except for a chest containing old photographs, drawings, school grades, and musical notes, everything could be thrown away.

We examined the cottage from the outside. The foundation was healthy, the ventilation worked as it should. The terrace was affected by dry rot, but that was easy to fix.

We heard steps and turned around.

A man was standing on the path leading to the other side of the cliff. He looked like a city dweller in his sailing shoes, white slacks, and expensive-looking woolen sweater.

"Can I help you?" he asked.

"Hello, I'm Markus Douglas. This is Carola. Sofia is, was, our sister."

He looked at us as if searching for some visible evidence of kinship but decided not to dispute it.

"Nobody's here," he said.

"I know. We just…" I made a sweeping gesture that could have meant anything.

He nodded.

"I understand. I'm sorry for your loss. An unfortunate case."

I nodded, and the man walked back to his own property.

I recognized the situation. You kept an eye on your neighbor's property, too. Strangers were not welcome in Porkkala. Strange cars, boats, and people were discreetly monitored. This was a refuge for the privileged.

While we were examining the new jetty, we discussed Sofia's death.

"Do you know anything about how she died?" Carola asked. "I'm sure she was a good swimmer."

"Allegedly she slipped on the stones and hit her head. If you lose your consciousness, it's possible to drown in just inches of water. Remember what happened to Ellen when she was little?"

"History repeats itself."

Carola remained silent for a while. "How was their marriage? Sofia and Arto's?"

"Like any middle-age marriage, I guess."

"Like yours?" Carola never was a pretender, and she wasn't subtle.

"Or yours," I said.

Touché. She shut up.

This was just fencing with words. Over the years, we had seen each other regularly, though more or less in secret, and we knew quite a lot about each other's lives. Our banter could seem a bit hostile, but it was our way of showing that we cared.

Nowadays our sibling fights had mostly been replaced by middle-aged civility.

Carola was divorced, but she had met Philippe five years ago, and they had some kind of short-distance relationship. They both lived in Paris, but in different districts. Philippe worked in a glass cube with an acronym on the door, something *International* and *Asset* and *Trust*, a hint of big money and tentacles all over the world. Carola ran her small but apparently lucrative architecture firm together with her friend Valérie.

We went to the sea cliff. When we were young, this was Ellen's favorite spot; she often played standing on the cliff. It was also one of our bathing spots. You had to know how to swim if you wanted to survive as there were many places where you could slip into the water. During winter, we sometimes plowed out a skating area on the ice. Some winters, my father made a hole or two for winter swimming or ice fishing.

The sea glimmered in the sunlight. The pines, the cliffs, and the sea were like they had always been. Gräspajkan Island, the rock of Stenskär, Madame Island a bit farther. No eider ducks; it was too early for that. I could smell the pines and the algae; I could hear the seagulls screaming. When we were children, we explored all the coves, every stone, every tree. We knew them all by heart.

"Nothing has changed," I said.

"Everything has changed," Carola said.

This was also the spot where Timo Auramo disappeared under the ice, a lifetime ago.

"Did you ever return here? After, you know?" she asked. Just as when we were children, our thoughts followed the same paths.

I shook my head. One summer, when I made a quick visit to Finland, Sofia invited me to Porkkala, but one of her children got sick, and she had to cancel.

"We should make a decision," Carola continued.

We had inherited the cottage from our mother, but only Sofia's family had used it as a summer house. Now that Sofia was dead, we had to decide what to do with the cottage.

We talked a little about Bellevue and a little about Sofia. We discussed the repair of the cottage and a possible splitting of the property. There were a lot of complex legal questions about ownership, transfer, and sharing of expenses, topics that were safe to talk about when you wanted to avoid something or there was nothing to say.

Carola had booked a table at an Italian restaurant in the center of Helsinki.

"I want to sell Bellevue," she said. "It's the only acceptable solution in this case. We have the right to redeem Sofia's share so we can make all decisions amongst us."

It sounded rehearsed. She articulated carefully, as if she had polished the sentence and was talking to somebody who didn't quite understand the language.

"Okay," I said.

She frowned. "You agree?"

"Sure. We'll do as you want."

"I wish you would be a bit more involved. Do you want to keep Bellevue for yourself?"

"Carola, I live in the US. I have no use for a summer cottage in Finland. On the other hand, I don't need the money, either. So frankly, I couldn't care less."

She inhaled as if she had come to a conclusion after careful deliberation.

"I will under no circumstances allow Sofia's husband and their children to keep it. Sofia's dead, I have nothing to do with them anymore."

Her tone was defensive, as if she expected solid resistance. That is something she used to do as a child, too; she always explained herself as if everyone was silently opposing her ideas.

"You are preaching to the choir. I know. They know. Everybody knows. We'll just sell it. Besides, Sofia's boys are grown up, they probably haven't spent their summers at Bellevue for years."

She nodded, not so much to show that she agreed, but to acknowledge that I had said something. She almost seemed disappointed, as if she had prepared her arguments in vain. She took a bunch of papers from her bag.

"I need a power of attorney. I have to visit the land register or whatever it may be called in this country. A power of attorney gives me the right to make agreements with the estate and with realtors, to sign contracts and such. Possibly we need to fix something before we can sell the property. If so, I will pay for it and then I'll deduct the expenses before we split the money."

"That'll be fine."

"Arto had the nerve to ask for compensation for the maintenance they have been doing over the years. Rather audacious. I laughed at him. They have been using the cottage for free, for thirty years!"

"Never underestimate a person's ability to forget inconvenient facts."

She went to the ladies' room, and when she came back, she had done something to her hair and to her face. I didn't know whether she had washed away the makeup or put on some more. Carola wasn't a vain woman, but she was aware of the impression she made.

We ordered a glass of wine in the bar.

I contemplated for a moment telling her about the letter I had received. Carola's son Max was twenty-five. My marriage with Debra remained childless, in the beginning to her grief, later perhaps to her relief. Now it seemed like I had an unknown daughter. I decided not to tell Carola about it, and that made me a bit uncomfortable. Even though we lived on different continents, we talked openly about most things.

Carola always became a bit philosophical when she had a glass or two.

"I have attended five funerals the last two years. Valérie's brother, the artist, you know, died of cancer. And Philippe's mother died last year. A colleague had a heart attack. Now Sofia. You know what I have realized? Money is not important, time is."

Like all fortune-cookie quotes and clichéd fridge magnet aphorisms, that statement contained a grain of truth, but I couldn't help laughing.

"You actually believe that?"

"Yes. This is something I have realized lately."

"And what do you do that proves you believe it? How do you use your time? Correct me if I'm wrong, but you use your time to earn money. You buy expensive shoes and bags. You drive your red sports car that you are so proud of."

"Markus, you are a nitwit." She said it as if she had just made a significant scientific discovery and wanted to share it. "Money is only a mean of payment."

She leaned forward.

"I don't want to argue with you. You're the only one in the family who is still talking to me. I don't want to lose you too. We have so little time, that's what I have realized. We have to manage time like we manage money. We can use it for something useful, we can invest for the future, or get something valuable. But often we waste it, we use it for unimportant things, and afterward we realize that the time is gone, we have no time left. And all we have, our memories, are superficial and of low quality. Like we had spent all our money on junk or technical stuff we don't need. This is what I have realized. Does this prove I'm getting old?"

I had no answer to that.

Had I wasted my time? Were my memories superficial and of low quality?

I knew what Carola meant.

My friend Bob Sheridan, who once was in charge of the South American zone, suffered a stroke a couple of years ago. Now he was paralyzed and communicated by moving his eyes.

My mother-in-law used to be a beautiful and intelligent woman; now she had Alzheimer's. She didn't always remember to eat and sometimes she didn't recognize her daughter or her closest friends.

Both were dependent on other people.

Sometimes I worried that I would be like that. Someday I could need someone. An unidentified spot on an X-ray, a strange reading from a blood sample. Neither my wife nor Miller would be helping me then.

My father always said that my sisters and I had to stick together. "You are the oldest," he told me. "It's your responsibility to take care of your sisters." I was only twelve minutes older than Carola, but he thought it meant something.

I was glad Carola existed.

She suggested we share a taxi to the airport the next day because our flights would leave at approximately the same time.

"So we'll have time to talk. Or maybe you could fly home via Paris. You could come and visit us, Max is in Paris now."

Home. Carola meant New York. Miller had used the same word, but he meant Helsinki. When you have lived abroad for a long time, home could mean a place you go to or a place you are coming from.

"Unfortunately there is no time for that. So much going on right now. I will probably be elected to the board," I said and immediately felt I as if was fishing for validation.

"The board," she repeated thoughtfully, as if she was looking for a synonym for a strange word. "That sounds great."

I tried to direct the conversation to something else by asking about Philippe and Max.

"The star constellations don't really exist," Carola said once when we were kids and she taught me about Orion, Cepheus, and Cassiopeia. She was interested in astronomy and the stars, and she knew almost all the star constellations in the northern sky. "We just see them that way, because looking from Earth, some stars seem to create a pattern."

Sometimes I feel like I'm also linking the bright lights of my life. When looking from a distance, they seem to be connected.

Ellen. Sometimes when I hear her name or see it written, I feel a short sting, like when a leg touches a nettle, hidden among dandelions.

Carola, whom our family abandoned.

Alison, of course.

Debra, my wife.

Ruby, the love of my life. I understand that now.

Sometimes I think there has been a meaning to all of this, that I have learned something. Sometimes I am sure I have learned nothing. Some things, of course, you only realize after the fact, when you can see how everything is connected. You can't connect the dots beforehand. You can only vaguely surmise that in the future there will be a clearly detectable pattern.

Part II

Alison

5

Ellen's favorite spot, the cliff, seemed almost like a raised stage. From there you had an open view of the sea, and on a clear day, you could see the whole Porkkala fjard. Ellen always brought her violin with her and sometimes she would stand on the highest spot of the cliff and play it, looking over the sea. The water carried the sound far away, even all the way to Upinniemi if the wind came from the right direction.

I can still hear the sweet sound of her violin. I can see her on the cliff, in the sunshine, her black hair loose. In my memory, she often plays "The Gypsy Girl's Dream," a simple but bittersweet and melancholic melody. That was the first actual piece of music she ever played. She learned it when she was four, and she played it her whole life. Sometimes I can hear her play Sibelius' Violin Concerto. She practiced it for the Sibelius competition the summer she was fifteen. The former piece is beautiful and tender, the latter dramatic and challenging. I still can't hear either without being transported to the shores of Bellevue.

As far back as I can remember Ellen always wanted to tag along with Carola and me and do the same things we did. She always carried her violin, hugging the case like a stuffed animal. When we stopped to pick bilberries, Ellen played. When we swam, Ellen played. When we played hide-and-seek, Ellen played, disclosing her hiding place by mistake. To us, her playing was like the noise of the seagulls, a sound in the background that we didn't listen to. Even Mother could sleep when Ellen played.

We treated Ellen like a kid sister should be treated. We loved her a lot and teased her a little. Once she could talk Carola and I tricked her into believing that she wasn't really our sister. We told her that we had found her on the island of Madame among the debris from a stranded Romanian cargo ship. She was lying on the beach wrapped in a sheet with a lifebuoy around her waist, and we took care of her because nobody else wanted her. She was a gypsy girl, we told her, and that was why she was so small and so dark-haired and such a skilled violinist. Ellen listened to our stories, her eyes wide open, and for many years she believed every word.

"I'm so glad that our family found me," she said. "Imagine if I had been found by evil people. I'm so…" and now she was moved to tears, "I'm so happy you found me."

She always wanted to hear more about her unknown relatives.

"Tell me about me," she would say when she wanted to hear something other than fairy tales. I invented wild stories about foreign countries. I told her stories about the caliph of Istanbul, about pirates from Saint Lucia and cannibals from New Guinea. Carola drew pictures of wild characters, dancing and playing, their hair long, their knives and violins black.

"Don't tell Mom and Dad," Carola said, just in case. "They are ashamed that you are not their child."

I don't know when Ellen realized that we had been joking. She never said anything, and even as a teenager, when she wanted to play the martyr, she would say, "Nobody cares about me, I'm just a gypsy girl."

Bellevue had gotten its French name because the original owner, Aunt Helena, the black sheep of the family, had been married to a Frenchman and she adored the view. The beauty, of course, was in the eye of the beholder. The landscape appeared barren—open sea, rock islands with no trees, granite—but to us it was exquisite. Our cottage wasn't the biggest or finest in the area, but we had the best location, we had our own bathing rocks and even a natural harbor that could have sheltered a small sailing boat. We didn't own a sailing boat, though, but we did have a rowing boat and a four-horse-power Seagull.

The day Timo Auramo's family moved into the cottage next door, Carola and I were eight and Ellen five. Sofia was a baby, so of course, she wasn't with us.

We were standing on the hill looking down when the Auramo car arrived at old Mattsson's property. A family with children had purchased it, and we knew they were Finnish-speaking and that they belonged to the Helsinki Southern Congregation, but the data about the ages and genders of the children were contradictory. We immediately saw that their car was a Mercedes-Benz.

A Mercedes.

We had a Simca, and most of the others in the neighborhood had Volvos or Fords, except for the Pursiainen family, who had a Volga. Nobody owned a Mercedes.

We had thought of asking Mother to bake a bilberry pie as a housewarming gift, but now we reasoned they would be so snotty with their fancy Mercedes that our bilberry pie and our company weren't good enough. The thought of it made us upset as if they actually had declined the pie, so we decided not to even acknowledge them. Carola suggested we throw rocks at their car when we got the opportunity.

But then Timo Auramo cut across the hill to our property, and he certainly wanted to learn to know us.

"I know who you are," he said in Finnish. "You are the Dewglas children."

"Douglas," Ellen said. "Not Dew-glas."

"Douglas," he humbly corrected himself.

Timo Auramo was three years older than Carola and I were, and he quickly assumed the role of leader.

We did things that I now, from a grown-up perspective, would call hazardous. Timo borrowed his brother's motorcycle and drove it along the winding road to the pilot station. It was, of course, illegal. We took turns sitting behind him, we never wore a helmet. Once we almost hit a deer standing in the middle of the road.

We liked going to the very end of the peninsula of Porkkala, where the sea was deep. During stormy weather, we stood on the rocks and let the waves hit our knees, and when the seventh wave came, sometimes it made us fall, and we laughed. The rocks were slippery, and the sea was deep, but we were excellent swimmers and our parents never worried about us. Occasionally we forgot about the time, and we would be gone for hours. Nobody asked about us. "Sometimes you have to accept a loss," Father would say. But he was joking. He knew that we watched over each other. That was rule number one.

When Timo heard our story about the abandoned child, he quickly got in on the joke and claimed that he had read in the newspaper about the Romanian ship and the unknown girl. He suggested we build a memorial on Madame, where we had found Ellen.

Many of the islands off the coast had different names on the map than the names we actually used. Anyone who used the names on the map immediately exposed himself as a non-resident. For example, Hamnholmen, Harbour Island, was usually called The Dead Man's Island, because once someone found a dead body on the beach. Madame's original name was Jungfruskären, Virgin Islets.

The name referred to the fact that the island was, in fact, two interlinked peaky islets, strikingly reminiscent of a pair of breasts. The eastern hill even had a small cairn that looked like a nipple. Between the two hills was a sandbank. You could wade from one island to the other as the depth was only a foot or two. The name of the island was Virgin Islets for hundreds of years until one October night during Prohibition. The Coast Guard was chasing an infamous smuggler in foggy weather. The smuggler knew the waters well, the Coast Guard didn't. The smuggler steered his boat between the two hills, shut off the engine, and let the boat glide over the sandbank. The boat touched the sand but managed to get over the bank. The Coast Guard had a much bigger boat, and it didn't stand a chance. Traveling at high speed, the boat hit the sandbank and got stuck between the two breasts, and there it stayed until morning when the fog lifted and the Coast Guard became the laughing stock of all the fishermen.

After that, the Virgin Islets were called Madame.

Timo created a monument by painting a rock red. He suggested we row it over to Madame.

Father had told us not to use the boat without him, but we still did it occasionally when he wasn't there. We would row to Gräspajkan Island or along the shore to the pilot station. We never used the Seagull. We would never have dared to row all the way to Madame by ourselves.

Now that Timo was with us, he assumed the responsibility. The weather was beautiful, the sea was flat, and we thought nothing could happen.

Together we pushed the boat off the beach. I was the last one on board. My feet got wet, and the boat rocked a bit when I pushed it and entered.

"Don't rock the boat," Ellen said. "That's dangerous. You'd better sit still."

We could see Madame off the cape of Upinniemi. When you looked over the fjard from the highest hills at Bellevue, Madame seemed close, but from the boat, the distance appeared surprisingly long.

Carola and I sat together on the middle bench, facing the stern, rowing with one oar each. Ellen was in the bow, her violin in her lap and Timo sat in the stern. The oars were long and heavy, and we were careful not to drop them. We glanced at each other to keep the pace.

The sea was almost dead calm, no waves, but the boat slowly heaved in the swells of yesterday's wind.

We had never been that far out by ourselves. To the south, we could see nothing but the open sea. Somewhere out there were the lighthouses and the shipping lane and even further south, the Estonian coast. We were heading to the west toward the profile of Madame and Stenskär Islands and Upinniemi. We could see our cottage grow smaller and smaller in the distance and when we were half-way, we couldn't even discern the sauna. This moment is etched in my memory. The illicit trip, our lunch box, the warm sun, the creaking oars, the feeling of freedom as our boat cut through the mirror-like surface.

We beached the rowing boat on the eastern islet of Madame. Timo positioned the painted stone on the highest spot of the islet, next to the cairn. Ellen was impressed by her memorial and played Mozart's "Turkish March" on her violin to celebrate.

Then Timo decided to play another joke on Ellen.

He claimed that it was possible to run on the surface to the other islet if your speed was high enough.

"Impossible," Carola said, and I agreed.

"But Ellen is pretty small," Timo said and winked at us. "She weighs next to nothing, and she's quick. If she sprints fast enough, she can run on the water as the swans do."

Ellen wanted to believe that, and probably Carola and I thought it was a harmless joke because the water wasn't that deep.

Tim counted fifty steps and placed a mark on the hill.

"If you start here, and run as fast as you can, your speed will be enough for you to run over to the other islet."

"Because of the surface tension," Carola said. That sounded convincingly scientific.

Ellen suspected nothing.

Timo was the starter.

"Ready, steady, go!"

Ellen shouted with pure happiness as she ran down the hill toward the sea, her black hair loose and her arms stretched out. She crossed the narrow beach and dashed into the sea, splashing water.

It was a windless day; the calm water looked like it was covered by the fragile first ice of the fall. For a moment, I thought that it might work. When you skip a stone, you can make it bounce off the surface if the speed and the angle are right. It didn't seem impossible that a tiny five-year-old could run a considerable distance on the water just because of sheer speed.

The water now splashed halfway to Ellen's knees. We already knew that it would never work, but we just laughed.

Then she slipped.

Under the surface, there were stones covered by seaweed, and her foot slipped. She fell backward, both her feet pointing toward the sky, her head disappearing under the water. Her head hit one of the stones with a nasty sound and then she was motionless, her face under the surface. The water slowly turned red around her head.

Timo blanched. Carola didn't make a sound. She just ran into the water with her clothes on and waded toward Ellen. I was frozen, unable to do anything. When Carola pulled Ellen out of the water toward the beach, my feet finally obeyed me, and I ran to help her.

We placed Ellen on her back on the sand. She was bleeding heavily from a cut just below her hairline and the seawater in her hair mixed with the blood and formed a thin film that colored her blouse and the sand red. She didn't move, but her chest rose and fell in an irregular rhythm.

We would probably have tried administering CPR, had we known anything about those things. Instead, we tied my shirt around her wound.

We did, of course, understand that we had to get back home as soon as possible. Tim wanted to start the Seagull, and we pulled the cord together, and the motor fired up. Halfway home, Ellen threw up, and we thought she would die.

Mother was awake when we came back to the cottage. Timo's family had a telephone, and we called for help. Carola and I took care of Sofia while Mother took Ellen to the emergency room in Kirkkonummi. The doctor shaved a patch of Ellen's hair and sewed the cut with a couple of stitches. When they returned, the rest of her hair was clotted together, the curls pointing in all directions. She had dried blood and sand, and even some seaweed on her blouse.

"You look like a troll," Carola said.

"I'm not a troll," Ellen said. "I was subject to a medical procedure."

She had bled heavily, but they told us that the wound was superficial and the only permanent sign of the accident would be a thin scar at the hairline.

"We thought you'd die," I said.

"I didn't die." Ellen yelped and jumped up and down to prove that she was alive. Then she stopped and frowned. "But I was hurt in my pride." She squinted and shook her head. "Pride is a deadly sin."

That's the way she was, Ellen. Sometimes it felt like she had a switch that in one position turned on a funny, precocious and almost drunk little girl and in the other position a concentrated, contemplative, and introverted philosopher or musician who always was afraid of missing out or being left behind.

When Father came home that evening, he didn't say anything at first. He looked at Carola and then at me. Then he looked only at me.

"Markus," he said. "This I didn't expect from you."

He said nothing more and I felt something in my throat, not because of the punishment I knew was coming, but because I once more had disappointed him.

Whatever Carola and I did, we did together, and we faced the consequences together. We had already decided not to disclose Timo's part in Ellen's accident. That was our own business, nothing that our parents had anything to do with. Father's rule number one was that we were supposed to take care of each other and rule number two was that you do not air your dirty laundry in public. If we had arguments—and we did, Carola was particularly good at arguing—Father didn't want us to tell on each other. He didn't want to know. The same principle applied to the whole family and to the congregation, too: private things were supposed to remain private. When Brother Sundquist stole the funds of the congregation and went to Sweden to drink it all up, Father didn't want the congregation to call the police, though there was a considerable amount of money missing. "The internal matters of the congregation are nobody else's business. Do not air your dirty laundry in public." He said that so many times that we often joked about it. "Do not air your dirty face in public," I would say with a fake deep voice when I washed Ellen's face in the snow. "Do not wash your dirty laundry in public," Carola would say when Mother put the laundry in a bag.

"I wonder how this could be," Father said. "You knew what I have told you about taking the boat, and you decided to disobey me."

I think he guessed that the idea was not only Carola's and mine. I assume that he appreciated us not telling on Timo. That's probably why our punishment was rather gentle.

"We are not like others. You know that. We don't lie. We don't steal. We obey our parents. Am I right?"

We nodded.

"Other people are worldly. They take drugs and listen to rock, they lie and steal and show no respect. But you know better."

We nodded again.

"You know what the Bible says about rebellious children."

We nodded.

"Well, what does the Bible say?"

"Whoever spares the rod, hates their children," Carola said and looked him defiantly in the eyes.

We had to cut the birch rod ourselves. It had to be thin and fresh and flexible. Father soaked it in salt water for a few hours. Then he made us stand in the family room and pull our pants down. Mother took Sofia in her arms and went outside. Ellen had to watch, her head covered in a bandage.

He hit us in turns, and we had to count the swats ourselves, one per year of age. The number of swats was always the same, but the implement depended on the offense. Sometimes a birch rod, sometimes a belt, rather seldom a thin electrical cord.

Carola and I took pride in not showing any pain, but when we put our pants back on, Ellen was standing scared stiff, pressing a wet fist to her mouth.

"Don't hit me," she said stamping her foot. "I'm just a little girl. Don't touch me."

It dawned on us that she believed she was about to get punished, too, even though she was the victim of our thoughtless joke. I felt a lump in my throat and forgot about the pain, and I hugged her. She never liked to be hugged or even touched but I held her close, and we cried together.

We never revealed Timo Auramo's role in the affair, but we thought it was unfair that we were the only ones to be punished.

We took revenge a few days later.

He was fishing at the cliffs of Draget when we sneaked up on him from behind. When he turned around and spotted us, it was too late. Though he was bigger and stronger than we were, he didn't stand a chance against the two of us. We dragged him down. He writhed and kicked and tried to bite, but we got him into the water. Carola sat on top of his stomach, and I pushed his head under the surface. He wriggled like a worm on a hook, and I saw the terror in his eyes.

Carola and I were capable swimmers, and we knew very well how long you could hold your breath. We waited calmly until a bubble revealed that Timo had given up and swallowed water.

We let him go.

He cried and coughed and vomited yellowish sludge. He lay for a long time on the beach, then got up and left, sobbing, without looking at us.

"We were never here," Carola shouted after him. "You slipped."

6

I was twenty-one when I moved to New York. There was nothing to keep me home, and I was offered an internship at the headquarters. Initially, it was meant to be temporary, and my visa didn't even allow me to take employment. Working at the organization's headquarters was considered employment under American law, so officially I was just a visitor, "invited to oversee tasks requiring special skills." The future was uncertain, but I was young, and I felt that the world was open and waiting for me.

I met Alison during my first summer in New York.

My mental image of New York was confused, because the map I owned was, due to technical reasons, printed with the avenues running from left to right, instead of down to up. Because of that, my initial orientation had a ninety-degree distortion. A familiar building would unexpectedly appear in front of me. I sometimes took the train in the wrong direction or turned left instead of right. Once I accidentally found myself outside the Public Library of Brooklyn, and that's where I met Alison.

During the first six months, I stayed with Bob Sheridan in a studio at 124 Columbia Heights in Brooklyn. Our apartment was on the sixth floor, and we could see the Statue of Liberty and the skyline of Manhattan. When I moved in, Bob presented the view like it was his personal accomplishment.

"Enjoy it as long as you can," he said. "You probably have to move out when I do."

Bob Sheridan was a couple of years older than me. He was myopic, intelligent, and he blushed easily. There was an odd discrepancy between his childishly round face and the three-piece suit he wore as if trying to gain an air of authority by dressing up. Like a first-year student applying for an executive position. He had worked at the headquarters for two years and was about to get transferred to an area where the need was greater. He was engaged and planned to marry as soon as the transfer was complete. I never met his fiancée who was living in Vermont with her parents, but he showed me a photograph of a plain but sweet, bespectacled woman who looked older than he was.

Our apartment was within walking distance of the headquarters, and I soon familiarized myself with Brooklyn Heights. But this one time I got confused. I turned south from Flatbush Avenue and was surprised to find myself in front of the Brooklyn Library.

It was one of those stifling hot August days in New York. I was in no hurry, so I got the idea of spending half an hour among books in an air-conditioned room. I crossed the roundabout, and there she was, sitting in the shadow on the stairs to the library, her knees pressed together, and a book and a bundle of papers in her lap, like a student waiting for class to begin. Her freckled face was shiny with moisture, and she had sweat spots under her arms.

I don't know what made me notice her. Perhaps it was because she was alone too or because she was reading a book or perhaps because she was directly in front of me. I pitied her a little. I could tell she didn't know she looked so sweaty.

She closed her book, and I stopped to get a glance at the cover. I didn't recognize the title or the author, but it didn't seem to be the kind of light summer reading a girl would read on the stairs when she's waiting for her friend, so I assumed she was a literature student. The idea interested me. None of the Americans I had met during the first few months ever read books. Of course, my interest wasn't only literary, she was attractive.

She looked up and saw that I was watching her. She swiped the back of her hand across her forehead as if she suddenly became aware that she wasn't looking her best.

"You're hot," I said to indicate that I understood.

It took a couple of seconds for us to register what I just said. Her face got one shade redder.

"No, I didn't mean that you are hot. Of course you are, but…"

I shut up. I was so helplessly tangled up in the double entendre that I considered it best not to continue.

I assume that I should've introduced myself with a confident smile and suggested that we find something to drink. Or perhaps I should have invited her inside the library to discuss books. Or maybe I could've sat down beside her and asked her name or what she was reading. Instead, I said, "It's warm in New York."

She looked away and smiled as if thinking of something private. I wanted to think that she wasn't laughing at me, but perhaps at an absurd thought that just occurred to her.

I smiled too.

"I have to go," she said and got up.

"*A Kodak moment,*" she later called this kind of situation, tiny moments when something happens, a decision is made, life takes a new direction. But at that moment I didn't do anything. She left, and I just stood there, on the stairs.

I began visiting the library regularly, even though I wasn't allowed to borrow any books. I had my passport, of course, but the librarian wanted to see an electrical bill or a gas bill to prove where I lived. I didn't know where to get one of those because my employer owned the building I lived in. And of course, I couldn't get any proof of employment as I wasn't really employed.

I just visited the reading room. I looked for the freckled girl, but I never saw her again, and after a couple of months, I had almost forgotten her.

7

When we were children, we didn't really understand that Ellen had a special gift or was exceptional in any other way. She just started to play increasingly difficult pieces of music until one day she was suddenly playing soloist for symphony orchestras.

When she was four, she abruptly informed everyone that she didn't want to play the piano like Carola and I did but wanted to learn the violin. Nobody knew where she got that idea from, but Mother, who at that time was in an active phase, arranged for her to get accepted into the music institute, even though the semester had already begun.

Ellen's first violin was a tiny sixteenth-size violin that looked like a toy. In the beginning, when she sawed the open strings, it sounded more like creaks than musical tones. We escaped outside or hid behind doors. But Ellen was persistent, and I'm sure that was an essential aspect of her gift. She had a knack for concentration and hard work. She tried to move the bow with the appropriate combination of angle, speed, and force. For a brief moment, she was able to produce a faint but distinct tone, and she wanted to repeat that moment over and over again.

"Don't look at your fingers, keep your back straight, your wrist flexible," she would command herself as she practiced in front of the mirror.

We didn't know then that Ellen had perfect pitch. She listened and imitated. When she tried to play her first melodies, her sharp ear helped her find the notes.

When I later discussed this with her, she told me that she could hear the sound in her head before her fingers reached the right position. She moved her fingers with minimal movements until she found the correct pitch. She was absorbed in her playing and could go on for hours and wasn't even frustrated by the fact that her hands were so small that it was impossible for her to play some of the pieces that her confidence tricked her to try. When she wasn't playing, she was still practicing. When she was on the bus, her fingers were playing an imaginary instrument, and she could hear the music in her ears. When she played with her dolls or painted with watercolors, the violin was playing in her head.

I have no memories of the time before Ellen was born. I've been told that when Carola and I heard that we were about to have a little sister or brother, Carola suggested that we get a puppy instead. But when Ellen was born, Carola could sit with her in her lap for hours. When Ellen learned to walk, we held her hands. When Ellen started to play the violin, I taught her to read notes.

Bellevue was our summer paradise, during the winter we lived in a high-rise area in the eastern part of Helsinki. One dark winter evening we were listening to the radio in the living room. It was a request show, and somebody had called in wanting to hear an aria from the opera *The Bohemian Girl*. We listened halfheartedly, with the radio playing in the background. Carola was drawing a galloping horse, I was reading comics, and Ellen folded clothes on her paper dolls. Sofia, the baby, was sleeping beside Mother.

"We'll hear a recording by the soprano Joan Sutherland," the radio announcer said. "This is 'The Gypsy Girl's Dream.'"

Ellen pricked her ears.

A few days later, when I opened the front door with the key I had on a cord around my neck, I could hear Ellen playing in the living room.

I immediately recognized the music, "The Gypsy Girl's Dream."

Ellen's memory was phenomenal. She had no problem remembering words, sentences, musical phrases, complete compositions. She played "The Gypsy Girl's Dream" flawlessly, by heart. The sound of the violin was delicate but solid, the intonation impeccable.

I listened, the melting snow dripping from my knit cap. I sneaked into the living room and sat down on the sofa with my outerwear on.

Ellen didn't see me. She was standing with her back to me, looking out of the window. This was the first time ever that I could hear her playing real music, not just a series of individual notes one after each other. She carved out the simple melody, let the violin breathe naturally, instinctively playing a small crescendo in the middle of the phrases.

My eyes filled with tears, but I didn't understand why, because I wasn't sad.

During the following years, when friends and family visited and Mother set out our delicate Arabia Myrna china, Ellen was the one who played for the guests. Mother accompanied her when at the age of six she played the Andante from Mendelssohn's Concerto in E Minor, or when at the age of seven she played *Csárdás*. The guests applauded her and admired her dexterity.

"I'm mature for my age," Ellen said, and everybody laughed.

Ellen's teacher realized Ellen's potential early on during the first lessons. While other children her age learned the notes and the parts of the violin with the aid of colors or childish metaphors—the bird string, the mommy string, the daddy string, the bear string—Ellen got increasingly demanding pieces of music to practice.

She was a hard worker but not always an obedient pupil. Once during a spring matinée, she performed an entirely different piece than her teacher had planned on because it "was a better fit." Another time, she "improved" a Mozart sonata by discarding a phrase and playing another, a positively non-Mozartian sequence instead. Often she would practice whatever she liked instead of what she was supposed to be practicing. When she was asked to play for our house guests, she did so willingly, but she never asked for requests. Instead, she played whatever she fancied at the time. During a phase when she was eight to ten, she got interested in jazz improvisation. She practiced that in secret because her teacher didn't approve. As a teenager, she developed a taste for bizarre atonal compositions.

Carola and I played the piano. We were mediocre, like most kids, but we were good enough to understand that Ellen was in a league of her own. Father was tone-deaf. He was skillful with his hands, and like Carola, he had an aptitude for mathematics, but Ellen's musical genes came from Mother. In her youth, she had been an accomplished pianist. She had won second prize in the Maj Lind Competition, she had received a stipend for studies in Berlin, and once she had accompanied Fischer-Dieskau himself when he still was virtually unknown.

When she met my father, she was a piano teacher and earned some extra money modeling for art students. Occasionally she got gigs accompanying classical singers, and she was considered to be going toward a brilliant future, but then many were.

In a way, it was because of Ellen that I got to know Ron Miller.

When Ellen was nine, an international assembly called The Victory of Truth was held in Helsinki. This was before special assembly halls existed, and most assemblies were held at rented ice stadiums or schools. This particular assembly was international and unusually large: we had thirty thousand delegates from twenty-four countries. It was held at the Helsinki Olympic Stadium.

In the attic of Bellevue, there is a faded color photo of our family outside the stadium. Mother is sitting on a bench with Sofia; everyone else is standing. Mother is small and fragile, Father is straight-backed. Carola and Ellen are wearing their new summer dresses, Carola in yellow, Ellen in white. I'm twelve, wearing a suit and a tie, I'm tall for my age, a miniature model of my father. Ellen is laughing at something nobody can recall. All of us have our name tags attached. Father is carrying a thin briefcase, Ellen is carrying her violin, and Mother has a couple of magazines in her lap as if she was about to go in field service from door to door. In the picture, we look like a normal family.

The assemblies were the highlight of our summers. Hundreds or occasionally thousands of people gathered in their best clothes. We listened to the program, watched the Bible dramas, exchanged experiences. As our congregation was small, this was the only time we could meet other children our age. Except for Barbara Anderson, Ellen's best friend, there were no other children our age in our congregation.

R. H. Miller was the principal speaker on Sunday. At the time, he wasn't a member of the Governing Body or even that high-ranking from a headquarters perspective. He was thirty-five or forty, but just the fact that he came from Brooklyn was noteworthy and valued. The initials stood for Ronald Henry, and when we later became good friends, I called him Ron.

We helped with the arrangements. We carried chairs, posted signs, decorated. There was a lot to do, but also hundreds of volunteers.

Ellen got tired of carrying things, and she opened her violin case. She tuned the violin with a couple of quick movements and started to play a brisk Kingdom Song. She was standing close to the entrance, under the concrete ledge, so the acoustics were not that subtle, but the reverberation amplified the sound, and the violin was able to overtake the background noise.

She played the first phrase as written. I remember she played it mechanically on purpose, as if she wanted to mock the simple melody. The then she started to improvise, to change the phrases. She sort of cut out small parts and pasted them back in the wrong places or played them backward. We knew the music well, so we spotted all the cuts and seams. Father frowned, but Ellen laughed out loud when she invented some ingenious combination. She added a few jazzy phrases she had learned from her records, and she increased the tempo. People started to gather around us.

Ron Miller arrived with his entourage. I recognized him from pictures. His face was round, he was of average height and somewhat corpulent, and could have been any random elder. But you could tell he was the leader; the others follow-ed him. He walked a bit imbalanced, wagging his cane, like a little girl not yet used to her high heels.

Ellen didn't notice him. I wanted to warn her, but she was so concentrated on her playing that she didn't hear me clear my throat.

Her music became wilder and wilder. Sometimes she let the phrase make a large jump and sometimes she let the notes glide into each other in a long glissando. At the same time, she emphasized the rhythm by knocking on the violin with her fingernails. You could still recognize the Kingdom Song in the background, but her version sounded more like a witch dance, wild, uninhibited, crude, like a crow among tropical birds.

Miller stopped. Most people around us knew who he was. Eventually, Ellen became aware of the change in the atmo-sphere, and she stopped in the middle of a phrase.

You could hear Ellen's tense breathing in the silence.

We glanced at Miller.

"Not bad," he said. "Not bad at all."

Everybody around us nodded, relieved. Sure, the girl was a brilliant violinist.

"But here's the thing," he continued.

He had a strange voice. It was almost a whisper, but a powerful whisper, hoarse in a peculiar way, like a blues singer who'd had a whiskey and now chatted between the pieces. But the voice was sturdy and piercing; he was a man used to addressing a large audience.

He held his hands as if he was demonstrating the size of a newborn baby.

"Somebody has created this music and written it down. Somebody who knows what is beautiful and what is fitting. That is the music we should be playing, not what is in your own little head."

He tapped Ellen on the top of her head as if she were the mischievous but ultimately well-meaning brat in the classroom.

I don't know if Ellen understood everything he said, but surely she understood the subtext. Her eyes flashed. I knew what she had in mind.

"Ellen," I said, but she pretended not to hear, and there was nothing I could do.

Years ago, she had discovered that her violin could produce sounds that reminded me of the sound you get when you scratch your nails on the chalkboard, a hollow, scratching sound that universally produces discomfort. Ellen knew how to generate several such sounds. She could position the wooden side of her bow close to the bridge or play a micro-interval on two adjacent strings.

Now she looked Miller in the eyes, played one of those extended, rusty sounds, made a dramatic bow, and put her violin away.

Father blushed in shame. He mumbled something, apologetically.

I don't know what came over me. Perhaps I remembered that Father once said it would be wonderful to shake the hand of someone from Brooklyn. Perhaps I tried to rescue Ellen from embarrassment and divert the attention away from her. I walked over to Miller and shook his hand.

"How do you do, Brother Miller, welcome to Finland, pleased to meet you."

I hoped my handshake was firm and confident. Miller said something, and I answered. I don't remember what we talked about. Probably we just exchanged trivialities. It's possible that he complimented me on my English.

One of the others pulled on his arm as if it was too early in the morning for this kind of drama. The schedule was tight; there was no time for this.

Miller turned around to leave. "Come over to Brooklyn one day," he said. "I'll show you around."

Later on, I understood that this was just typical American politeness, but I was twelve, so I took him at his word.

8

It was ten years before I saw Ron Miller again and one more year before we met in person.

My workplace was in the Squibb Building that used to be the head office of a medical company and recently had been converted into our headquarters, but I had nothing to do with the management and never met anyone from the top floors, let alone anyone from the Governing Body. Sometimes I saw Miller's name on some internal notice, or as the signee when someone was appointed to a new position. Miller worked in the Writing Department on the eighth floor, and he was expected to be elected to the GB, our disrespectful name for the Governing Body. Miller was still young, fifty at this time, and all the men in GB were old. The youngest was sixty-five and the president of the organization, K.H. Norrman, was almost eighty.

From the main building, it was a short distance to High Street from where you could take the A Train to Manhattan. Our printing facilities were close to the station and were connected with the other buildings by covered bridges and tunnels under the streets.

Initially, my job was about the automation of the printing presses. The offset system had to be configured and calibrated, and that was something I had learned to do when working for the Frenckell print shop. But after a few months, I mainly worked on improving the phototypesetting. The methods of the time did not allow for easy changes of character set or font size, and our goal was to be able to print books in different languages on the same press. For that purpose, we had developed a multi-language electronic phototypesetting system called MEPS.

This was a time when computers were water-cooled and big as printing presses. In addition to the mainframe computer, we needed smaller controllers, and because no commercial microcomputers were available, we had to build everything from components that we purchased in electronics shops. Jay Levine and a couple of other electronics experts built the computers. I didn't know much about the hardware, but I knew how to program. Bob Sheridan and I were responsible for the testing of the central mainframe system.

My work wasn't intellectually demanding. I punched holes in cards in order to instruct the computer to print ready-made text passages on lithographic paper. The texts were nonsense, just *lorem ipsum* — dummy texts. The paper was then converted through negative film to printing plates made of aluminum. I ran through the tunnels to the printing facilities on Adams Street, checked the output, adjusted the parameters, and repeated the whole process.

We were strangely revered by many of the others. They thought there was something marvelous and extraordinary in being able to make a computer obey your instructions and we didn't rectify the delusion. Others assumed that we created a program that automatically translated from one language to another, and usually, we didn't correct that misunderstanding either.

When the introduction day for newcomers was held, I had already been working in Brooklyn for two months. The head of Human Resources gave a lecture in the morning. We took a tour of the facilities, then we were divided into small groups to discuss various themes, and we had lunch together. In the afternoon, we sat in the main auditorium.

I immediately recognized Ronald Henry Miller when he walked onto the stage. The same sharp eyes, the same erratic walking style, the same hoarse whisper that now sounded almost terrifying when magnified by the microphone and the speakers.

Bob had told me that Ron Miller had had his tonsils surgically removed when he was young and he had been ordered to be totally quiet for some time after the operation. But he had had an argument with someone in the headquarters — rumor had it that his adversary was the president of the organization — and Miller permanently ruined his vocal cords. In addition, Miller had some kind of chronic inflammation that made it difficult to walk. The disease was named after a person. I joked that it probably was Portnoy's Complaint, but Bob couldn't remember.

Miller started by explaining the rules in the Branch Organization Procedure.

"There are 28 subjects and a total of 1177 policies and regulations. We are expected to follow them."

There were rules for just about everything. You were not allowed to discuss your work with coworkers, and obviously not with outsiders. Married couples who worked in different departments couldn't talk about their jobs with each other. You couldn't discuss books that hadn't been published yet. Private visitors were only allowed after hours. If anyone was in a room with a member of the opposite sex who wasn't a close relative, they had to leave the door wide open. There were rules for the length of skirts and the lengths of sleeves.

"It's a matter of showing respect to the organization and to each other. During hot summer days, it's not necessary to wear a suit, but a short-sleeve shirt is not appropriate. That would make us look like a politician on holiday, and we want to avoid that."

Then Miller talked about women.

"Many of you have only little experience with women. One should hope," he said.

We laughed politely.

"The woman is the weaker vessel, but that doesn't mean we can treat them like they were of lesser worth. It's true that many women tend to gossip and some of them act like they have power or like they think they are men, but we do not tolerate any derogatory labels. Trolley dolly may seem innocent, but we want to avoid that expression too."

Bob Sheridan had explained the phrase to me during the first week. A trolley dolly was a young, attractive sister who delivered the internal mail or coffee and sandwiches with a metal cart. Like a flight attendant, he explained. If the sister wasn't attractive or young anymore, the accurate label was cart tart. Bob continued with a whisper, "And if she's even older, she's a wagon dragon."

In the fall, Bob Sheridan was relocated to San Miguel de Allende in Mexico, where there was a fair number of English-speaking foreigners. Bob wrote a couple of letters, but after a while, we lost contact. Many years later, I heard that Bob had founded the first English-speaking congregation in Mexico.

Since Bob had moved out, I had to move out too. The room was intended for those who were employed at the headquarters, and because of my visa problem, I wasn't one of them. Instead, the internal rental agency helped me find a room at Willow Place, within walking distance of Columbia Heights. It was a typical Brooklyn brownstone with fire escapes down to the street. My room had a window on the shadowed side on Joralemon Street. There were three other rooms on the same floor. Our shared bathroom was in the hall. The landlady lived in the same house, and she rented exclusively to single men.

"No ladies in the room," she said.

There were more than two hundred congregations in New York, but luckily I was assigned to one close by, the Farragut congregation on Adams Street. There were others from the headquarters assigned to the same congregation, but they seldom attend the meetings. One of them was a member of the Writing Committee and Ron Miller's colleague. That was the reason why Miller got to hear about my first talk, and that greatly influenced my work in the headquarters and later affected my whole life.

During my first year, they cut me some slack because I was a foreigner, but once my English was considered adequate, I had to give talks like everyone else.

I had given talks since I was ten, as soon I was tall enough to reach over the lectern to the microphone. I had given talks about the pagan practice of celebrating Christmas and about the ancient Greek words for love: *agápē, érōs, philía,* and *storgē.* I never read straight from the paper; I only had the most important words written down. When I was fifteen and my voice already was a man's voice, I once dropped my notes when I walked to the stage. I had to improvise the whole talk from my memory. But the talk was a success. The brothers and sisters complimented me on my enthusing and exciting talk. "It sounded almost like a real talk," Ellen said.

My first talk in the Farragut congregation was about whether we could choose which Biblical principles we wanted to follow. The answer was obvious.

I started with the standard phrases and cited some Bible verses, but for emphasis, I developed the line of reasoning with an example and let the talk follow its own path.

"Imagine," I said, "that a housewife is baking bread."

I could immediately feel that I had a grip on the congregation. Everybody's eyes were on me. These short talks adhered to ready-made outlines, and you weren't supposed to change anything. Now the con-gregation sensed that I digressed and that was interesting. An exception was always interesting.

"When we cook, we should follow the recipe. Somebody has invented it and knows what kind of ingredients we need. Each ingredient has a purpose; everything counts. Imagine that our housewife reads that she'll be needing flour, salt, water, and yeast. Yeast? she asks herself. It doesn't taste like anything, or maybe it tastes bad, and we don't need much of it. The yeast doesn't seem to have a function. Perhaps our housewife's independent thinking and her worldly wisdom make her conclude that the bread will be as tasty, or even tastier, without yeast."

The congregation laughed. Even those who had never baked bread realized by the way I presented it that it wasn't a clever idea to bake bread without yeast.

"What happens? Is the bread any good?"

I paused and let my eyes gaze over the audience.

"When we question a teaching we don't understand, we are as foolish as that housewife. There are things we do not understand the importance of because we don't have all the information. There are things that we as imperfect humans cannot ever grasp. Does that mean that we can decide for ourselves which principles to follow? Or should we listen to the guidance the organization gives us?"

People tend to focus on motion, so it's usually a good idea to employ gestures when giving a talk. I spoke slowly, without large movements, but I connected the ideas I expressed by using small distinctive hand signals as if picking them from the air. I separated and summarized. I would put one argument in my right hand and another in my left hand, and with a small wavy motion, I would make one of them seem silly and elicit a burst of laughter. Now I had their undivided attention, and it was time to finish. I paused and pointed at my Bible.

"This is not a McDonald's menu. We can't point at whatever we want and simply discard what we think we don't need."

A couple of weeks after the talk, I got an invitation to see Ron Miller. I had no idea what Miller wanted to discuss. Did he remember me and wanted to say hello? Had I been guilty of some unknown offense?

I took the lift to the eighth floor. Behind a small table, the brother on duty checked my name on a list before he accompanied me to the end of the corridor.

When I stepped into the room, Miller got up from his chair, took his cane in his left hand, and shook my hand. He had a handshake of steel.

"Brother Douglas, nice to meet you," he said in his hoarse voice. "You are probably a bit surprised by this invitation."

"Brother Miller, it's an honor to—" I said but he interrupted me.

"I've been to Finland once. Lovely country."

He gestured me to sit down.

He didn't remember me. It wasn't surprising considering that it was almost ten years since we had met and I had been twelve. He hadn't changed much, but I had grown to be a man.

A trolley dolly knocked on the door and brought us coffee.

There was a mechanical toy on Miller's table with metallic spheres that bounced into each other. Only the first and the last ones bounced; those in the middle remained still. It had something to do with kinetic energy and communicating bodies. I thought that Carola probably had a scientific explanation for the phenomenon. While the trolley dolly was in the room, Miller said nothing, he just set his toy into motion and stared at it.

When the girl shut the door, Miller cut to the chase.

"Your talk has attracted attention. Do me a favor, will you? I'd like a copy of the talk."

"A copy? I don't think anyone recorded it."

"The text, Brother Douglas. I want a copy of the text."

I explained that I hadn't written it down word for word, only a few bullet points.

He considered that for a while. "But surely you remember what you said. I want a transcript. It doesn't have to be verbatim, but I want the main points, especially the parable of the housewife and the bread."

I promised to try. He looked at me for some time. He got to his feet. "I didn't ask you to try. I asked you to write."

I didn't know what to say.

"You may borrow a typewriter. Say, Friday?"

I had to borrow a cart to get the typewriter home. It was an IBM with a typeball instead of individual typebars, and the whole thing weighed three times more than my father's old manual Olivetti. But it was electric, and it came with two alternative typeballs with different fonts.

First I wrote a quick version of my talk because I wanted to capture all my thoughts on paper and I didn't care about typing errors. I made corrections with a pen, drew circles around sentences and passages I wanted to keep and arrows to show where to move them. Then I rewrote everything, double-spaced. The next morning I put the typed pages in an envelope in the internal mail.

I almost forgot about it.

Three months later, there was an article in our magazine about how important it was to follow the guidance of the organization. My story about the housewife and the bread was in it, practically word for word. "We must follow all instructions we receive, even if we don't like them or they do not seem to make sense," was the final sentence.

I kept the typewriter. Nobody asked for it, and I never returned it.

As a child, I enjoyed writing little stories on our Olivetti, and now I resumed that hobby. I bought a book with ten-finger typing exercises, and after a month, I typed fifty words a minute, flawlessly.

Later I came to realize that writing is my way of figuring out what I think. Only when the words are on the paper, do I believe in them. Many people have considered me an excellent speaker, but words are easily forgotten, and a passing thought can always be dismissed as a passing thought. The written word is the truth.

I wrote my little tales in the evenings. Perhaps one could call them short stories, but I know now that they weren't that good. I still keep them in a folder. Some of them are embarrassing, others innocent. Some are about Ellen. I wrote them in English, and that proved to be excellent training because when I later got additional writing assignments, I didn't need to look the words up.

9

Ellen wasn't cross with Timo Auramo after the accident on Madame, and soon we were all friends again. Ellen even admired Timo, and sometimes I was a bit jealous.

Timo was practically a member of the family. When Mother was tired, he carried water from the well and helped her cook. He knew how to change Sofia's diapers and how to tar the boat. One summer, he grew two inches, and his voice sometimes broke when he spoke. I felt like a little boy beside him.

Timo didn't speak any Swedish when they bought the cottage in Porkkala, but since many of the children in the area were Swedish-speaking, he soon learned the most important expressions and understood almost everything, even though he always answered in Finnish, like Mother. This was not a problem; we used whatever language felt best. Some phenomena lay in a gray zone and could be expressed only by borrowing an expression from the other language. Sometimes we changed the language in the middle of a sentence. Ellen believed for a long time that all fathers spoke Swedish and all mothers Finnish.

One day we were sitting in the car on our way back to Helsinki when she asked why Timo wasn't living with us in the city.

"Well, he lives with his own family," Mother said.

"But he's our half-brother," Ellen said.

"No, he's not," Carola said. "We're not even related."

"I know," Ellen said. "But I wish he was our brother. And if you wish for something really hard, it's half true."

I secretly wanted the same thing. Sometimes I regretted that I had no brother, just three sisters. Nothing wrong with sisters, but there were things I would have liked to do or talk about with a brother. I knew what Timo appreciated and adapted my own opinions according to his so that he would consider me an equal. Timo had two older brothers whom we didn't have much to do with, but the fact that he had brothers meant that he knew things about motorcycles and engines and — something we understood later — about sex.

In the high-rise area of Herttoniemi, our family was anonymous, almost nobody knew of our faith. But in Porkkala the situation was different, all the families knew about each other. Then again, we were in no way unique. The Silbersteins were Jewish, but not very orthodox; the children didn't even attend the Jewish school. The Bergmans and the Pursiainens were ordinary Protestants but didn't go to church every week. We weren't sure about the Soisalos.

"They are Catholics," Father said with a voice that put them under the same label as rapists, drug addicts, and rock artists, but Mother claimed that they weren't really Catholics, just normal Finnish people who happened to belong to that religion.

We children didn't care much about that. There were many children our age in the cottages around Bellevue and we visited each other whenever we wanted. The difference between the groups wasn't so much what we did; it was more what we didn't do. The Silbersteins didn't eat pork, we didn't celebrate birthdays or Christmas, and the rest didn't attend meetings or assemblies.

Since Timo belonged to the same faith, Father thought Timo was a good role model. Timo readily took the initiative. Timo could teach me responsibility. Timo would one day become an elder.

"It wouldn't hurt if you were a little more like him," Father said.

Father had a firm opinion of what boys should be like. I pretended to be interested in nautical charts and in servicing the engine, and Father pretended that I was good at crafting wood, but we both knew that if Carola hadn't been a girl, she would have been the next construction engineer in the family. She was the one who wanted to learn how to use a fretsaw, and she was the one who took the alarm clock apart to figure out how it worked.

Father was mostly annoyed by the fact that I read too much and the wrong kind of books at that. In Herttoniemi, there was a library close to the school, and I visited it every week. In Porkkala, there wasn't any library, but a bookmobile stopped at the store once a week. I read Biggles-books, Hannu Salama, Enid Blyton, Kipling. I wasn't aware of the differences in style and quality, I simply devoured everything. If I had no access to books, I read old newspapers or the text on the oatmeal package.

Sometimes on summer nights, when my sisters had fallen asleep and the sounds of Bellevue had subsided, I slipped up to the attic. My flashlight consumed batteries at a rate I couldn't afford, so probably I didn't read in secret that many nights, but this is how I want to remember it: I read every night, sometimes into the wee hours.

You could reach the attic by a narrow staircase and a hatch-way. At both ends of the attic, there was a window. The one to the southwest had an open view to the sea. The attic was cramped and sultry, full of old books, newspapers, notebooks, and photographs.

Most of it once belonged to Aunt Helena. We avoided talking about her and pretended that she never existed. She was disfellowshipped from the congregation before Carola and I were born. To be disfellowshipped was the worst of fates: in an instant, you lost all your relatives and your friends as if they all had died in the same disaster. What Helena had done, we never really understood, but like children who become aware of things never articulated, we understood that we weren't supposed to ask any questions about Helena. To us, she wasn't a person, she was a mythical non-person, a ghost you scared children with. "Helena will come and get you if you don't do as I tell you," Mother would say when we were little, and we were terrified.

In the attic, you could find evidence that Helena once had lived—photographs, letters, books. She had been married to a Frenchman and had lived in Paris before she bought the property and had Bellevue built. Our mother inherited Belle-vue after her death. In the attic, there were old volumes of *Paris Match*, books by Scott Fitzgerald in English, by André Gide in French. The name inside the books was written by a Francophile: Hélène Routala Donnadieu. Carola said that Hélène was pronounced almost like Ellen. Carola was curious about this unknown relative, and she studied the old letters in secret and chose French as her first foreign language in school.

I was mainly interested in Helena's books. At the time, I couldn't read English very well, let alone French, but the covers of the books intrigued me, and I borrowed the translations from the library. Some of them I read to Ellen, too.

The first time I saw a printing press was when I was twelve and visited the Finnish Branch Office with Brother Weckman. Father was on a business trip, and Brother Weckman assumed responsibility for me and suggested that we first go in field service together and then visit the Branch Office in Tikkurila.

"I'll show you the new annex and then the press," he said.

He'd only invited me, but Carola had to take care of Sofia, and I didn't want to leave Ellen by herself, so I took her with me. We waited together for Brother Weckman's Volkswagen at the bus stop.

Brother Weckman didn't say anything when he saw Ellen, but when we were driving toward Tikkurila, he explained how the Branch Office needed both brothers and sisters.

"Remember, women feel while men think. Men have more practical minds, their brains are better at directing and organizing. Thus the supervision of women by men is God's arrangement. Do you understand?"

I nodded warily.

"But Carola is smart," I said. "And Ellen is talented."

"I'm sure they are. Women frequently measure up to men and surpass them in intelligence. But a woman cannot lead a congregation. There are many women at the Branch Office in Tikkurila, but they are doing female things, they clean, they cook. A man shouldn't do what a woman can do, and a woman shouldn't do what a child can do. Markus, you will grow to become a man. One day you may be a circuit overseer or give talks at assemblies or serve at the Branch Office."

The annex had recently been finished, and everything was new and shiny. The asphalt on the parking area was glossy black, and around the building, there were flowers and automatic irrigation. Inside, you could smell the fresh paint on the walls. Brother Weckman showed us the canteen, the meeting hall, and the accommodation area.

Then we visited the printing facilities.

Even though everything else was brand new, the presses were old. That day, press number two wasn't in use. The old rotation press had broken down and spat out large sheets of paper that filled the whole two-story space as if a giant toilet paper roll had rolled out by itself. There was chaos, a great deal of cutting and folding and shuffling of paper.

Ellen let go of my hand and dived into the paper and skipped and jumped and yelled.

"Ellen," I said with an apologetic look at Brother Weckman.

"We'll get rid of this old junk," the brother who was in charge of press number two said. "As soon as we get the funds, we'll get offset."

Offset was something that they talked about at every meeting because donations were always needed.

In the other hall, press number one was in operation. It spat out a constant stream of paper that in the next phase would be cut into books.

Brother Weckman introduced us to the brother in charge.

"I'm Ellen," Ellen said. "I'm a girl. Markus is my brother, he'll become a circuit overseer one day and he'll be giving talks at assemblies and he'll serve at the Branch Office."

The brother in charge smiled at me in admiration of my brilliant future.

He told us that one rotation of the cylinder produced four new books.

"Isn't it enormous?"

I nodded and pretended to be impressed by the sheer size of the press. I had no interest in the mechanical side of the printing process, I mostly felt sickened by the noise and the smell of chemicals. But I was fascinated by the thought that somewhere someone had written a text on a typewriter and then, after a complicated and multifaceted process, that text appeared on a print plate, and these thundering behemoths printed, cut, and glued thousands of books out of it. And much later, at a different location, someone read one of these books.

When Ellen was in the fairy-tale stage, Mother was often tired and Father was busy, so it was my duty to read to her. She was able to read music when she was four, and she recognized some written words like her own name or the words allegro or decrescendo, but she needed my help to read books. I enjoyed her overt admiration of my ability to decipher the small letters and magically create stories out of them. I read not only children's books to her, but sometimes middle-grade or even adult books. That's probably why her vocabulary was expanded with unusual, complicated, adult expressions. For the most part, she used them correctly.

When I didn't have access to books, I invented my own stories, but I never knew beforehand how the story would end. I just made everything up as a talked, so sometimes the stories were not that coherent. But Ellen never complained about plot holes and accepted without complaint the wild leaps I had to make to make it all fit together.

Sometimes my stories would be about my sisters. My model was the famous stories about Emil of Lönneberga, but my heroine was a girl called Ella.

"I did not," Ellen claimed when I told her a story about how Ella borrowed the neighbor's cat and washed it in a bucket with a dish brush and detergent. The cat hid under a drawer and didn't come out until the next day.

"But the story is not about you, it's about Ella."

"I'm so little," she defended herself. "You can't demand too much from me. Besides, the cat was dirty."

One day, I told her a particularly exciting story. It was about three sisters, Carina, Ella, and Soffe, who lived all alone in a house. Their parents were dead, and their brother was abroad. I made the story up while I told it and the result was a gruesome ghost story that ended with the girls finding a skeleton in the basement.

Ellen hid her face in her hands.

"I'm scared now," she whined, "and it's not just because I'm a child. That story is horrible. Tell it again!"

I told it again. Now that I knew how it would end, I changed it a little in the beginning and hinted about the existence of the basement long before it was needed in the story itself. Even Carola reluctantly admitted that it was a rather creepy story. I told it to Timo, too, but he just laughed.

That evening I wrote it down using our typewriter.

I learned to read when I was five, but I have no recollection of how it felt when I understood how the letters formed words. But I remember the Olivetti. I pressed the key—you had to press forcefully—and the letter appeared on the paper. If I pressed the letters in the correct order, I could write complete words, and it almost looked printed.

I wrote the ghost story with two fingers. I made a couple of small changes and carefully put the sentences together so that you could read the story in a monotonic ghost story voice. The typewriter was broken, it couldn't write the letter "k," so I meticulously left an empty slot each time there was supposed to be a "k." Later I penciled in each "k" in the right spot and tried to mimic the font of the typewriter. It took hours just to write the "k"s.

I showed Father the pages. He quickly read them through. At first, he didn't say anything. He had taught us that if you can't say anything nice, don't say anything at all.

I felt a lump in my throat. Father gave the pages back.

"You have gone to a lot of trouble."

Later that evening I was sitting in my reading corner in the attic and heard Father talking with Mother. It was a discussion not intended for my ears, but it was about me.

Father was a man of principles. In addition to Catholics and women wearing trousers, he despised sailboats that were too big and luxurious, music that sounded like the orchestra was just tuning up, books containing made-up stories, and more than anything, weak men.

That was rule number three: a man was supposed to be a man.

"I don't know what to do with Markus," I heard him say. "He's worthless. How can he ever become an elder?"

"But Gunnar, he's only a boy."

"He invents stories. He has a vivid imagination, and it's not getting any better by him reading so much."

"Markus is just sensitive. That's not a bad thing."

I don't know how long I stayed in the attic. I must have fallen asleep because suddenly I realized I was cold. The house was silent, and the early sun had woken up the seagulls.

10

Ron Miller had got it right; most of us didn't have a lot of experience with women.

It was hard to make contact with American women. In our congregation, there were only two girls of my age, and I wasn't interested in either of them. Quite a few young women were working at the headquarters, but most of them were married, and it would have been inappropriate to try to interact with those who weren't. It wasn't forbidden to have a conversation as long as you weren't behind closed doors, but it definitely wasn't appropriate to initiate a conversation over the gender barrier without being introduced first. There were no women in our department. Next to the coffee maker, there was a sign: "No sisters are working here. Wash your own cup." My only interactions with females in the headquarters were with a few trolley dollies and Sister Powell at the internal post department who always greeted me by my first name. "Good morning, Brother Markus." It's possible that she thought my last name was Marcus.

Outside the office, there was an abundance of worldly wo-men. It was surprisingly easy to talk to them because they often took the initiative. But it was hard to get any further. A couple of times, I tried to ask for a telephone number. I assumed that was what you were supposed to do, but the only number I got belonged to the Bronx Zoo.

But this one time I got into a longer conversation.

It was a late evening. I was allowed to use the laundry services of the headquarters, but it was a rather long walk, so I preferred the laundromat around the corner. I always brought a book, because the mute television that hung from the ceiling only showed sports or soap opera reruns. I seldom talked to anyone. But this evening I chatted up a young woman. Her hair was in a ponytail that protruded through the hole in the back of her basketball cap. She was also engrossed in her book and didn't look up until her washing machine had finished the cycle. She refilled it, showed me a five-dollar bill and asked me if I could give her change.

Our hands touched when I gave her the coins.

"Happy families are all alike, but every unhappy family is unhappy in its own way," she said and looked at my book.

I nodded, appreciating that she knew the beginning of *Anna Karenina*.

"What are you reading yourself?" I asked, and she lifted her book.

It was something by an American author I didn't know.

Her name was Stacy, she was twenty-one and from Ohio. She was studying to become a teacher.

"At Columbia?" I asked because it was the only New York university I knew.

She frowned as if wondering if I was serious.

"Long Island University, Brooklyn campus. And you?"

"I work with computers in a...well, it's a print shop, or you could call it a publishing company."

We were encouraged to witness spontaneously to strangers, but I didn't want to scare this girl away.

We talked about books and compared our reading habits that weren't exactly opposite but still different. When I told her that I wrote short stories for the drawer, she told me she did that too. When my laundry was done, it was nearly one in the morning. We were alone in the laundry, except for a homeless person sleeping on the chairs.

"What was your name again?" she asked when I emptied my washing machine.

"Call me Markus," I said to test her. I wanted to show off a little, too.

"Okay, Ishmael," she said, and we laughed.

I decided to wait for her washing cycle to finish.

"I think this is where you should ask me to come and have a look at your short stories," she said when she emptied the last pieces of clothing from the dryer.

That hadn't even occurred to me, but now that she mentioned it, it seemed like a good idea.

We took our bags and walked toward Willow Place. When we dashed over Atlantic Avenue, she took my hand, and I let it happen because the risk of somebody seeing us was practically non-existent.

"I love your accent," Stacy said as we left the big street and took one of the smaller ones. "It sounds like chopping wood. Behind the Iron Curtain."

She pushed her jaw out and made her vowels hollow and change the th-sounds into z's and the w's into v's.

"I zink ve shoud go home now, togezer," she said. "Into ze night. I luff you."

I thought it sounded like a Russian or German accent and felt a bit dejected. She sensed that and squeezed my arm.

"I like your accent, I really do."

Before I opened the door, I told her that we had to be quiet because the landlady would flip out if she heard a female voice. Stacy stifled a giggle.

I looked through the drawer in search of a suitable text.

"This story is six pages long. It's about a young girl who gets to play an expensive violin."

She took the pages with an amused smile, as if prepared to say something dismissive. She glanced at the first page, browsed a little, and started to laugh.

"You actually invited me here to read your short stories."

"I thought you were interested," I said. I tried not to show that I felt a bit hurt. Her laugh was friendly, but her reaction surprised me.

She approached me and touched my cheek.

"Of course I'm interested, honey."

She stood on her toes and kissed me. Her lips were cool and moist.

"I think you are the most innocent creature there is," she said. "Or else the cultural differences are just too…"

She took her laundry bag. I could hear her laugh on her way down the staircase.

It was more than a year before I met Alison again.

I visited the library often but had long ago stopped looking for the freckled girl. But one spring weekend, I attended the assembly of the neighbor circuit, and during the first day of the assembly, I saw her.

It was an afternoon, in the middle of April. The assembly was held in a rented school close to Prospect Park. The mood resembled those during the assemblies of my childhood, not really lighthearted, but full of expectations. Happy people everywhere, children, families, young women walking in pairs.

I had volunteered as an attendant because I had already heard the program. The admission to the assembly was free, but sometimes apostates or homeless alcoholics tried to get in. Sometimes people simply had the wrong address. That's why everybody had a name tag—it was easy to see quickly who belonged.

During a break, I stood outside the building with my hands behind my back and kept an eye on the crowd. I noticed a girl walking past me, on her way to the shadowy area. She had neat assembly clothes, a newly ironed shirt, a pleated skirt, high heels. I didn't initially make the connection to the sweaty literature student, but when our eyes met, she gave me a coy smile and nodded.

This time I knew what to do. I held my arm out and stopped her. She read my name tag, and I read hers.

"Would you like to…" I said and nodded in the direction of the cafeteria.

"I do," she said solemnly and then we both realized what she had said and she blushed and we laughed and the ice was broken.

I don't remember much of our first conversation. We probably talked about general and trivial things, but at the same time we put out feelers, testing the ice, trying to break it. We laughed at the coincidence that we had met a year earlier without having a clue that we almost belonged to the same circuit.

Before we parted, I asked for her telephone number, and she wrote it down on a program leaflet that she then folded and put into my pocket.

"Give me a ring," she said.

I didn't know what to think. She noticed my bewildered reaction.

"A buzz. A call," she explained and made a fist with the little finger and the thumb pointing out. We laughed again.

I called her the following day, and on Saturday, we had a date. I think you could call it a date, for lack of a better word, because we just took a walk in her neighborhood. The rules stipulated that we should have met in a larger group before meeting on our own, but I didn't have a large circle of friends. Bob had already moved out, and I didn't like to spend my spare time with my colleague Jay Levine.

In the beginning, Alison was watchful, tense, like the deer at Bellevue when they scented the air, still, ready to flee. We walked side by side along the broad street toward the tip of the peninsula. I listened to her and instinctively understood that she was talking too much to cover up that she was nervous. It made me feel surprisingly warm to realize that I made someone nervous. Our conversation skipped from one subject to another, returned, deepened all of a sudden, got sidetracked, lingered at mutual experiences.

She told me that she was born upstate; I told her I was from Finland.

"Finland," she said. "Sounds exotic. Cold, but exotic."

That's the way she was. She tasted words and names, gave them surprising adjectives and categorized everything according to how it sounded. Markus sounded like spice, she said, like rough slanted surfaces, like thick flannel, open fire, like log cabins.

I listened to her childhood memories and got to tell my own in exchange. She asked about my siblings, and I told her, but not everything. I hesitated to tell her what Carola had done and that I still stayed in touch with her, but decided to take the risk. Alison said that not everything is black and white.

"You are doing the right thing," she added.

I liked her way of saying my name. She stretched the "a", and when I pointed that out, she corrected it, and now it sounded like a dog barking, and we laughed together.

We crisscrossed the streets of south Brooklyn. We stopped once for coffee. Every now and then we had nothing to say. This interested me. Even when we said nothing, the silence wasn't awkward.

There was an older sister in our congregation called Alison Delaney, and I started calling her by her full name, just to have an excuse for saying the name. "Use it in a sentence," my English teacher always said.

I became aware of my appearance. I started to iron my shirts. At work, when we sorted out a problem with a data run, Jay Levine joked as he usually did. When I didn't react as he expected me to, he asked if everything was all right.

"You are so" —he chose the word deliberately—"absent-minded."

I felt busted. I said something about being homesick.

He suggested that we go for a beer after work, but I hesitated.

"I insist," he said. "Of course you have time. Bros before hoes, you know."

He made a pantomime with his hands. Breasts and hips.

He asked who she was and I vehemently denied there was a she and wondered how I could be so transparent.

Carola called. She asked about our parents and about Sofia, but there wasn't much to tell. I told her that Mother was ill again. She pointed out that I had mentioned the name Alison at least three times during our call.

"Who is this Alison?" She laughed, but it was a friendly laugh.

I called Alison a couple of times when I knew she was working because I wanted to listen to her answering machine. Her message was airy, her voice was clear, and in the background, I could hear laughs and clinking of glass and china.

11

Usually, when you think back to past times, the details dissolve. It is difficult to say exactly when something happened. You have only vague memories of certain events, the chronology and the specific year have disappeared somewhere into the depths of your memory.

Sometimes you remember things wrong. I recall that Carola was wearing her checkered dress when Ellen had her accident, but a photo proves that the dress was bought the following year.

Sometimes I remember a photograph that was taken at a specific time, but I have forgotten what happened right before or right after. I don't always know if I remember the event itself or just the photo. In my memory, they are the same thing, interchangeable.

In the photo albums at Bellevue, there are only a few photographs from our early years. Carola bought a camera when she was sixteen. All photos before that were taken by others. The oldest are black-and-white, some are Polaroids, the newer ones are faded quadratic color photos with a white frame. Sometimes there are years between the pictures. Our life seems to be a series of undocumented events, occasionally punctuated by random events captured with photographic sharpness. What lies between, years of undocumented life, is invisible to posterity. The photographs don't lie, but they crop reality.

In the albums at Bellevue, there are no photographs of Ellen's untidy room, of Aunt Helena, of disastrous family dinners. The images document selected moments, assumed to be important. Weddings, parties, travel. But the significant moments, the moments of minimal changes, when surprising chord changes occur, when life takes a new turn, those moments are never captured.

There are exceptions.

There is a picture of Ellen and Barbara Anderson when they are seven and eight. Barbara's mother took it. Ellen is carrying her violin case, and Barbara is standing, looking at her. It's possible that this is the precise moment when the girls meet for the first time. Barbara has just participated in the music institute's entrance examination, and Ellen is on her way to her music lesson. Barbara's mother takes a picture of her daughter, and Ellen is captured in the same photo, more or less by chance. We discovered the coincidence a few years later, and we got a copy of the picture for our family album.

A few months after the picture was taken, Ellen began going to the same school as Barbara. The girls first met in the Music Institute and then in the schoolyard. They became best friends.

Then Barbara and her mother joined our faith.

I used to do field service going door to door with my father or with a brother from the congregation. Carola, Ellen, and Sofia usually went with an older sister. Mother was irregular; she seldom shared in door-to-door ministry and sometimes got reprimanded for that.

We gathered on a street corner in Herttoniemi for the meeting for field service. The elder read a few lines from the magazine and then led us in prayer.

"Dear heavenly Father, we once again turn to you in gratitude. We thank you for guiding us with your organization, and we thank you for letting us be your witnesses so that we are able to tell our fellow people about your Kingdom and give them the possibility of salvation. We pray that you let your Holy Spirit guide us and that you bless our work. In the name of Jesus, Amen."

Everybody repeated Amen.

Then we decided on work teams and territories. Father and I were assigned to the apartment buildings at Majava Street. I got to take the first door.

Although I never admitted it, I despised taking part in the door-to-door ministry. I felt uncomfortable ringing the doorbell uninvited, trying to get the householder to buy a magazine or a book or a tract. Some listened politely to my introductory phrases and then found an excuse for not having a discussion. Others shut the door as soon as they saw us.

I always hoped that nobody was home when it was my turn to ring the bell. Mostly I was afraid that the person opening the door would prove to be someone I knew, like a classmate or a teacher from the Music Institute.

Someone opened the door.

"Hello, my name is Markus, and this is my father. May I interest you in a Biblical question? Do you know that the Bible has predicted that the wicked word will come to an end and we all can live in an earthly paradise?"

I knew the passage by heart and had my finger on a suitable place in the Bible should the person allow me to read.

"Aren't you Ellen's brother?" Barbara's mother asked.

She invited us in. Father took the lead and told about the blessing God had in store for mankind after he had destroyed the present wicked system of things. Barbara's mother was a widow and when Father talked about how God in the new world would wipe out every tear and death would be no more, and neither would mourning nor outcry nor pain be anymore, Barbara's mother listened attentively.

A few weeks later Barbara and her mother started attending our meetings. We were enthusiastic about the opportunity to have new members and treated them with warm, overwhelming kindness and love. They made great progress, and soon they were involved in the congregational activities. We called them the new Andersons because there had been another Anderson family before.

There must have been a lot to marvel at and perhaps a lot to digest. Our Kingdom Halls were simple; there were no crosses or crucifixes, no stained glass. Not everyone took communion, just a select few, once a year during Memorial. We had no priests, only elders and overseers dressed in suits, like businessmen. Meetings three times a week. You had to engage in the door-to-door ministry. Young boys got to give talks, to learn public speaking. Girls didn't give talks, but they gave small two-person demonstrations, teaching each other. A woman couldn't teach a man; the other person had to be another woman or a child. Our religion was called the Truth; all other religions were called Babylon the Great. In the magazines, there were pictures of Paradise with smiling families patting lions and in the background, there were a candy-colored lake, a waterfall, and a snowcapped mountain, coned like Kilimanjaro, or Fuji.

As violinists, Ellen and Barbara were on entirely different levels.

When Ellen was seven, she was already the rising star of the Music Institute. After her first year, she got a new teacher, a Hungarian pedagogue called László Király—he pronounced his last name KeRYE—and she began to attract attention among those in the know. Special arrangements were made, exercises were tailored, violins and bows were carefully selected, important persons were invited to follow classes and nod approvingly. Ellen was also the indirect reason why László Király founded a string orchestra for children. To be able to develop as a musician, he claimed, a young violinist needs experience in chamber music at an early stage.

Barbara was a sloppy player, her pitch was constantly a bit flat, and she wasn't admitted to the string orchestra. But she never showed any envy. Ellen was her idol, and she seemed genuinely happy for her when Ellen became a soloist on an international level in her teens.

Timo Auramo didn't understand music at all, but he appreciated speed and acceleration and incredulously shook his head when Ellen, at the age of ten showed off with that passage in Paganini's Caprice no. 24 where the left hand plays pizzicato. The bow bounced off the strings, and Ellen's fingers moved so fast that it was impossible to see what she was doing. Timo asked her to play faster and faster, and there seemed to be no limit to how fast she could play. Once Ellen and I competed at who could play the *Flight of the Bumblebee* by Rimsky-Korsakov the fastest. She played her violin, I played the piano. She did it in sixty-three seconds, flawlessly. When I tried, I couldn't manage even a minute and a half.

"Ellen ten. Markus zero," she said.

Ellen was of course technically proficient, but she also had a unique ability to bring out the essence, breaking up the music into pieces like building blocks, in particular when she improvised over a theme. Sometimes she and Barbara played together. Barbara played a simple melody and Ellen improvised over it. Sometimes she would play a completely different melody, a pop tune or a folk song above Barbara's melody, like a second voice, and oddly enough, they always fit together.

"How do you do it?" Barbara asked. "How can you possibly know that two melodies fit together?"

"I don't know," Ellen said. "I see the notes as colors. I just mix them into new colors. Mostly they represent nothing. But sometimes they do."

Barbara was by nature taciturn and pensive and didn't come forward with her own views but always agreed with Ellen, much the same way I agreed with Timo. Ellen talked the same way she played, linking unexpected things together, skipping from one subject to another. Father said she wasn't concentrating, but I think she just made surprising but logical associations. For example, when she found out that Carola at the age of eighteen had a secret boyfriend, a certain Simon Goldberg, she bought her a twenty-year-old record she had found in a second-hand shop on Albertinkatu Street. The sleeve was immaculate, and the record itself didn't have a scratch. The gift was Ellen's way of teasing and saying, "I know, I approve."

It was a recording of Bach's *Goldberg Variations*.

"Just wait until you're eighteen yourself, then you'll understand," Carola said and hugged Ellen, who was a head shorter.

"I must live through you," Ellen said. "I'm too young to have a life of my own."

That record was the only personal object Carola took with her when she left us.

*

Barbara visited Bellevue in the summer and once her mother also came. We served grilled herring and coarse rye bread, and toward the evening Father suggested that we a take a trip out to the sea. The weather was suitably calm and clear, and he wanted to show us the sunset.

You could see the sunset from Bellevue as well, but not really, because the trees of Upinniemi were in the way. Father said that if you see the sun descending in the water, you can see a short green flash just when the upper edge of the sun slides below the horizon.

That was him. His actual job was to figure out how thick the concrete reinforcing bars, the beams, and the pillars were supposed to be so that the houses he built would not disintegrate in a cloud of crumbled concrete, but his real passion was nature. He taught us everything about the weather, about birds, about the sea. We could distinguish a great black-backed gull from a lesser black-backed gull, crowberries from bilberries. We were familiar with wind directions, high pressures and depressions, cumulus and cirrus clouds, Beauforts and barometers.

"Stand with the wind at your back," Father explained. "Stretch your left arm diagonally forward. That's where the low-pressure center is. Now look up. If you can see high clouds, check in which direction they are moving. That's where the low pressure is moving. If they move to the right, the wind will turn clockwise, if they turn to the left, counter-clockwise. If they are coming toward you, the wind will increase, and the weather will be getting worse."

Or:

"If the swallows are flying low, it means the insects are flying low. That means that the air pressure is low and the humidity is high. Then it will soon be raining."

He explained how all places on earth get an equal amount of daylight per year. At the North Pole there is sunshine around the clock during summer and no sun at all during winter, while in the tropics the day is divided into two equal parts.

"How do you know all this?" Sofia asked. "Is it because you are an adult and we are children?"

"Fathers know everything. You can't become a father unless you pass the test."

"But what happens if you don't pass the test?" Carola asked. Of course she didn't believe it, but she wanted to play along.

"Then they get to be the mother," Ellen said, delighted by her own wit.

Mother and Sofia remained at the cottage because the boat was too small for everyone to fit. The sun was already low when we headed out into the shipping lane, toward to lighthouse and over the fishing shallows and further out over the Finnish Gulf, bypassing the rocky Kallbåda. Barbara's mother wasn't used to boats. She anxiously looked back to the shore that was moving farther and farther away. When the mainland disappeared under the horizon, Father shut down the engine.

We were out early. The sun was setting but still hovered a bit over the horizon.

"The sun will set in half an hour," Father said and showed us how we could figure that out. He took Barbara's mother's hand and sat down next to her so that they could look in the same direction. He held her hand up toward the sun.

"Stretch out your hand and count how many fingers can fit between the sun and the horizon. One finger is fifteen minutes. Now you can fit two fingers, so the sun goes down in about half an hour."

We all raised our hands toward the sun.

"My fingers are thinner than yours," Ellen said.

"But your arm is also shorter. Try it, it works every time."

He was right. My, Carola's, Ellen's, Barbara's, and Barbara's mother's hand-operated sun clocks all indicated half an hour.

There was no wind. We were in the middle of a high-pressure area. The sun's reflection glittered in the water. As the sun approached the horizon, it seemed to move more quickly, and soon it was half-way under the horizon. We stared at it. We didn't want to miss the quick green flash. It would be an exquisitely beautiful and unique moment.

We waited until the sun had set. We never saw any green light. When the sun sank deeper under the horizon, only a darkening glow remained. Dew formed on the benches. In the direction of the mainland, you could see blinking lights from lighthouses, buoys, and the lanterns of boats and ships.

"Civil twilight," Father said. "That's when there still is some light, and you can't see the stars yet. After that comes the nautical twilight, when the horizon is still visible, and the brightest stars light up. Finally the astronomical twilight. Then it gets dark."

Father started the engine and headed back toward the Porkkala peninsula. At Stenskär Island we turned toward Bellevue. We could see the warm glow of the cottage windows. Mother and Sofia had prepared an evening meal and were waiting for us.

Father knew where the underwater rocks were and even though it was dark, he didn't hesitate for a moment. He steered past the rocks, around Gräspajkan, turned the engine off and let the boat drift of its own speed up on our little sandy beach.

12

Alison lived in an apartment close to the Brighton Beach sub-way station. The bottom floor windows had security bars that curved around bulky air conditioning units. I didn't know much about Alison's neighbors, but on her floor lived a Russian couple and a young man who sometimes tried to sell me a watch or a car stereo. I had seen Heather, Alison's roommate, only in passing. They had their own rooms and shared the kitchen and the bathroom. Heather's room was strictly functio-nal. Instead of a painting, she had hooked up a t-shirt. Alison's room was more girly, full of floral and sparkling stuff and on the wall hung a poster from a wildlife conservation organi-zation with images of cute and furry animals with big eyes and worried expressions.

One day we took the subway to the Bronx and found our way to City Island. It was Alison's idea. The island was diffi-cult to reach from Manhattan and therefore not particularly attractive to tourists, but those who came, came precisely be-cause there were so few tourists. Alison described the place as a piece of New England in the middle of the big city, with picturesque wooden houses, fish restaurants, jetties and mari-nas, nothing grand, no mansions for the rich, just ordinary homes for ordinary people, each with their own beach and a sea view, a paradise in the heart of the city. I got the feeling that she was exaggerating as if she didn't trust her descriptions to be sufficiently vivid. I wouldn't have cared if City Island had proven to be a shanty town. I just wanted to be with her.

We took the train to Pelham and continued by bus. We walked from the bus stop to Tony's Pier, ordered fish soup and sat diagonally to each other so that we both could look out over the water and the boats.

Alison wanted to sit in the shade. She was wearing a light summer dress, and I noticed that she had freckles on her shoulders. She had freckles on her breasts, too, but that I found out later.

"I have to tell you something," she said seriously. "Just sit quiet and listen. This is not easy for me."

I said nothing.

"When I was eighteen, I met a man. Patrick was nineteen and from another congregation. I knew him through mutual friends."

She fell silent but didn't look at me.

"You can guess what happened. We were together for six months. Then Patrick got remorseful, and he confessed to the brothers. We almost got disfellowshipped."

I was in the habit of joking with her, so I thought of getting up with a frown and pretending to ask for the check, but I saw that she had tears in her eyes. I nodded to show that I understood.

"I was forced to move because of the shame. Here in New York, nobody knows me, but the brothers know, of course, since all my papers were sent to my new congregation."

She fell silent. I considered saying something, but she raised her hand to stop me.

"I wanted you to know. But I don't want to know anything about your past life, you are here now, and that is all that counts."

In the evening we arranged an impromptu picnic on the roof of Alison's house. We had wine and bagels and grapes. We didn't think of bringing candles, so we sat in the dark, wrapped in blankets and looked at the black sea where tiny lights revealed the location of the ships. We listened to the traffic and to the muted noise of the waves. The salty smell of ocean mixed with the aroma of the wine and the bread.

I told Alison about my short time in prison, how conscientious objectors belonged to the highest caste among prisoners. We were almost at the same level as those convicted of economic crimes, significantly higher than rapists and child murderers. I told her that my time in prison was mostly just boring. Alison squeezed my hand.

I told her how I had wanted to show my texts to the girl from the laundry, how embarrassing it was when I didn't know how to read a woman. Alison chuckled and gave me a kiss on the cheek.

I told her about Ellen. I told her things that I never told even Carola. I told her about the last summer, about the violin competition, about the party, and about Timo Auramo's drowning.

Alison said nothing and I was grateful for that.

I stayed over for the night and lay down beside her in her bed.

I wondered how you would go about it for the first time. Maybe there was some sort of code that everyone was supposed to know how to manage the embarrassing moment when both parties waited for the other to make the first move. Maybe the more experienced one of us had to pretend to be inexperienced and maybe I, who in fact was inexperienced, was expected to take the initiative and play according to rules I didn't know. I was afraid Alison would weigh me on a scale calibrated by Patrick and find me to be lacking.

The whole affair was clumsy and a bit sweaty, our bodies moved in opposite phases as if we danced to different types of music. I was too quick, the end came without great drama in an unexpected wave, as if a plastic swimming pool for children suddenly had ruptured.

I felt a complex sensation of simultaneous disappointment, pride, gratitude, and shame.

"Don't worry," Alison said.

So many times I had lived through this moment, known exactly how I would feel, what I would do. And now the abysmal gap between expectation and fulfillment. My failure and Alison's empathy.

She curled up in my arms and stroked my shoulder.

"Markus," she said.

I didn't want to reply; she knew that I could hear her.

"Will you respect me in the morning?"

Her voice was full of laughter, and I laughed too, though perhaps I laughed too much.

Later we lay in each other's arms. She hummed to herself, and I recognized the tune. It was the melody Ellen used to play as a kid, "The Gypsy Girl's Dream." I joined her humming, a bit surprised that she knew the song. I think she was surprised I knew it, too. The last phrase she sang out loud.

"But I also dreamt, which pleased me most, that you loved me still the same."

Her voice was frail but beautiful and then she taught me the lyrics to the whole song.

It was the end of May. Alison wanted to show me something, but she wouldn't tell me what it was. We took the subway to Manhattan and stepped onto the bridge at the Pan Am Building where Park Avenue crossed 42nd Street. Pedestrians weren't allowed on the bridge because it was intended for cars going to or coming from the tunnel, but still, there was a large group of people. Everybody seemed to be waiting for something, all looking west.

"This only happens twice a year," Alison said. "And today the weather is clear."

We watched the sinking sun. 42nd Street goes a little bit uphill at Fifth Avenue, then goes a bit downhill toward the western river bank, but since we had a high vantage point, we could see the whole street all the way to the Hudson River and New Jersey's low profile.

It was a matter of minutes before the sun would set. I remembered how many years ago, on an August night, we had tried to catch the green light. I assumed that Alison was expecting something similar and didn't bother telling her that it was highly unlikely that we would see it.

The sun descended between the skyscrapers, and then I realized what was about to happen. There would be no green light—the interesting thing was the position of the sun. The sun rays beamed together in a strictly focused point. The sun was positioned in the middle of the canyon formed by the skyscrapers, fully aligned with the Manhattan street grid. As the bottom edge of the sun touched the ground, all the perspective lines converged simultaneously in the middle of the sun. The setting sun glittered on windows and windshields, metal surfaces reflected the orange and the yellow and the red. This was something that would occur only today; on no other day would the sun set exactly in the middle of the street.

I marveled at the impression. It was as if this wasn't a random phenomenon, but something that was preplanned when Manhattan's street grid was designed. I was thinking of Stonehenge, of sundials, and Mayan calendars.

All of us on the bridge shared the unusual experience, admiring what nature and human interaction had achieved by coincidence. Then the sun sank below the horizon, and the city lights and the blue shades took over. The traffic below us was unaware of the spectacle. Traffic lights changed, cars honked, New Yorkers rushed to do their important errands.

I think this was the exact moment when my mental map of Manhattan finally became aligned with the surrounding reality. I knew where I was. I didn't need any green light. It all came together, and I was in the right place at the right time.

13

Carola, Ellen, Barbara Anderson, and I all went to the same school, though Carola and I were assigned to parallel classes. Carola was a conscientious and reserved schoolgirl, always at the top of the class. She wrote rules and instructions to herself and timetables that she meticulously followed. Ellen was an extrovert, stubborn and careless. She ignored her homework and gleefully skipped school whenever she wanted. She had the energy for music; everything else was marginal.

Ellen and Carola were opposites in other aspects too. Carola, like me, had inherited her looks from our father: we were blond, tall, and slender. But Ellen resembled Mother: she had straight, virtually black hair, a fine-boned, almost bird-like physique. She had a small red mark on the chin—typical for violinists—and an endearing gap between her front teeth.

Carola was Daddy's girl. When she learned to write, she wrote small letters on pieces of paper that she hid in his pockets or his suitcase when he was going on a trip. They were written with capital letters, like a kidnapper's ransom letter.

Ellen and I were close. She wore my old t-shirts as nightgowns, because she liked the smell, she said and giggled. She was perceptive about my moods. She told me her secrets and reached for me when she needed help. I defended her in the schoolyard if anyone messed with her.

Carola was uninterested in her appearance, while Ellen was childishly fond of beautiful clothes. She stood in front of the mirror and did things with her hair, she cut out pictures of fashion shows and movie stars, and spent her weekly allowance on glass and plastic jewelry. In Carola's room, everything was neatly in its own place, but Ellen's room looked as if a princess in a hurry had emptied all drawers and cupboards in search of something small and valuable that she had lost.

Ellen was easily impressed by everything she read or heard about, and she sometimes confused fantasy with reality. She tended to exaggerate and invent stories. Mother warned her that one day she wouldn't be believed, even if she told the truth. Sometimes when she wanted to stay home from school, she claimed that there was no school that day and when she got caught, she maintained that she had believed it was a school holiday. Once she was "absolutely certain" that she had seen a corpse in the swamp at Böle, though there was nothing to be seen when we checked it out. A year earlier, an American girl, an exchange student, had drowned in the swamp and rumor had it that it was a suicide. Ellen was fascinated by this and began to see corpses everywhere.

Ellen not only liked beautiful clothes but luxurious houses too. When we took a walk in Marjaniemi or Tammisalo admiring the fancy mansions with their swimming pools and jetties, she would earmark this or that house for herself, after Armageddon. She was particularly fond of a pink gingerbread house near the Laajasalo channel.

"Little girls can't choose," Carola said. "The brothers at the Branch Office will choose first, then the elders and finally the ministerial servants and the pioneers. You may get a tiny cottage."

Carola and I thought a cottage would be nice, but Ellen wanted marble and iron gates and a sea view.

"We could choose a bigger house the three of us," she said. "We could live there together. And Sofia as well. Everyone would have their own room, and we would have a garden and a jetty and a boat."

Even though Carola and Ellen were different in many respects, they would gang up together if needed. They were girls and knew, or thought they knew, things that boys didn't have a clue about. They would glance at each other at the dinner table and giggle at things we knew nothing of.

Sometimes Carola and I banded together. We had our secrets and code words. Father's rule number four was that he didn't tolerate vulgarities, so we developed our own profanities. When Ellen got older, she was initiated.

"Railway sleepers," I said once when I dropped my ice cream cone in the amusement park.

Carola giggled, she knew what I meant.

"What does that mean, railway sleepers?" Ellen asked.

"I'll tell you later," I said and glanced at Father.

Ellen wouldn't forget such a thing, so as soon as we were out of earshot of our parents, she wanted to know. I had a habit of not giving her the answer directly, because I wanted her to find it herself.

"Translate railway sleeper to Finnish," I said.

"*Junalankku*? I don't get it."

"Choose another word."

Ellen frowned and tried to find a solution to the riddle. Then she gave up and her eyes filled with tears.

"You have to explain it to me. My thirst for knowledge is so profound, and I'm ill-equipped to understand such things on my own."

Carola took mercy.

"*Perkiöllä on junalautoja saatavana,*" she said in Finnish. There are railway sleepers in Perkiö.

She pronounced the sentence neutrally, without emphasizing anything. But Ellen had an acute ear, and she immediately understood what was implied by the first syllables. It sounded nearly identical to "*perkele jumalauta saatana*": *Goddammit, Satan the Devil.*

Ellen mastered both languages equally well and enjoyed the pun and the fact that she was in on the joke, and for several days she cursed incognito whenever the opportunity arose. Father asked a couple of times what we meant by railway sleepers, but we just looked at each other and giggled. Many years later, when I was living in the US, I learned an American version. *Cheese and crust, got all muddy — Jesus Christ, God Almighty.*

My parents never used profanities, of course, not even when they were arguing. Instead, they were deliberately respectful; the politer they were, the more dangerous the quarrel. Sometimes it was about a strange receipt or a wedding ring that was supposed to be on the finger but surprisingly was found in a pocket. Sometimes it was about a suitcase forgotten in the wrong hotel or about train tickets to places nobody was supposed to be going to. Everything was sorted out during bedchamber trials that ended in war compensation agreements: perfume bottles, Toblerone chocolate, large bouquets of roses.

Once Mother had cooked lamb. Of course, we didn't celebrate Easter, but we did have lamb during the days surrounding Memorial. Mother cooked the lamb in the oven for too long, and the temperature was too high—she was sloppy when it came to following recipes—and the lamb was almost black. We had to strip out a thick layer of burnt meat to access the edible parts.

"Your charming mother has gone to a lot of trouble in order to make sure that we don't have to eat raw meat," Father said and chewed ostentatiously. "You can't get meat this well done, even in the finest of hotels."

Mother stopped chewing.

"Your father is admirably sympathetic to our modest meal considering how much fun he had when he was away."

They were talking to each other but through us, as if the other wasn't even present.

Father said nothing, just continued to eat.

"Won't you tell your children, Gunnar, how much fun you had on your 'trip?'"

She pronounced the last word so that we could hear the quotes.

"Dear Anna, we are eating now." Father's voice was neutral, but there was a trace of warning.

"Apparently your father thinks this doesn't concern you," Mother said and looked at us.

"Apparently your mother thinks it's appropriate to discuss work at the dinner table."

Mother smiled.

"Really, work? Ask your father if it was boring sitting in a hotel room all evening. And ask him how come Brother

Lassila calls him at home when he's traveling with Brother Lassila."

"Anna," Father said through clenched teeth.

"I'm too little for this kind of stuff," Ellen said sullenly. "I'm just a child."

"Or am I wrong?" Mother continued. "Do I simply have a vivid imagination?"

"Enough is enough."

"That's it. I just imagine things. I'm emotionally unstable, and I'm projecting my own problems upon you. I apologize, I won't disturb you further."

The bedroom door closed with a bang.

"Let's eat now," Father said.

"This meat is tough," Sofia said.

"That's just the way it is, we have to be content with what we have."

"Let us all be grateful for God's undeserved kindness and this abundance of nourishing lamb meat," Ellen said piously.

"Ellen," Father said.

There was silence for a couple of minutes as we ate what we could. Then Ellen opened her mouth again.

"This lamb was probably called Helena," she said and glanced at me.

Here we went again. Ellen's uncanny ability to find surprising connections in mundane things. I tried to stifle a giggle, but unfortunately, my mouth was full of milk, and I squirted some over my plate.

"Markus, please. Not at the dinner table."

But now Carola and Sofia laughed aloud too.

Father banged his fist on the table.

"Could you be kind and explain to your father what's so funny," he said and stared at Ellen because she started it.

We sat still. The Helena joke didn't seem funny anymore. The thing with quick and witty associations is that they never work if you have to explain them.

Father waited.

"The lamb was called Helena," Ellen said softly, "because it's the black sheep of the family."

We waited for Father's reaction. He did have a sense of humor, but it was difficult to predict what made him laugh and what by some unwritten rule was inappropriate.

I could see a small movement in the corner of his mouth, though he tried not to show it.

"Let's eat," he said. "Not a sound from any of you, or else…"

He pretended to be angry.

"Or else we'll be brought out to the gate of the city and we'll be stoned to death and the ravens of the valley will peck our eyes out," Ellen said solemnly.

Father banged his fist again and roared.

Ellen's lip trembled.

"My big mouth is going to get me into trouble," she whispered to me.

14

Often we don't appreciate things until they have become memories. It's a pity Carola never met Alison. I have a feeling that they would have liked each other, the earthy but emotional, talkative and sometimes endearingly insecure Alison, and my intelligent, but reserved and somewhat clumsy sister.

Alison's store didn't open until ten on Saturdays, but I had to get to the office, so I woke up early and jogged along the ocean. I took a final sprint up the stairs. I turned on the coffee maker, showered, shaved.

Alison was already awake. She smelled so warm and newly awakened that despite the risk of being late to work, I crawled back beside her.

The sheets were cool. Her skin was warm.

When I reached climax, something startling happened.

A warm wave spread through my whole body, from my head down, an intense and clear wave that took my breath away. It became stronger, reached its apex, and lingered as a slowly dying afterglow. I felt as if I were outside my own body, I felt heavy and relaxed and warm, and to my immense surprise, I realized that even though I had come countless times before, I had just reached my first orgasm.

When I had had breakfast and left, it wasn't even seven o'clock yet. I left Alison sleepy and content in her bed and went out in the summer heat in my newly-ironed white shirt. My heart was light and happy, and the train arrived at the station exactly at the right time.

I was consumed by my thoughts and looked out of the train window. In the southern parts of Brooklyn, the train ran above street level, and I could see far over the roofs, down to the street, into the houses. Puerto Ricans, black people, white. Streets and shops, millions of people, millions of lives.

Only when the train approached Brooklyn Heights and our headquarters, it went underground, and there was nothing more to see.

This was my third summer in New York, and everybody at the headquarters was talking about the purge of the ninth floor.

The president's nephew, Vic Raymond, who was a member of the Governing Body and the head of the Writing Department, had quietly gathered a number of well-known and influential brothers around him and had tried to get them to either overthrow the Governing Body or establish an entirely new religion.

Ron Miller disclosed the plan. He'd had a conversation with Vic Raymond about some doctrines that were to be included in a new book and noticed that Vic Raymond was an apostate. Miller secretly taped a couple of conversations.

Before the summer assemblies, we learned that Vic Raymond had been disfellowshipped. For the first time in history, a member of the Governing Body had been expelled. The mere thought of it was unimaginable.

The hunt for Vic Raymond's accomplices was in full swing at all levels. They were found on the ninth floor, they were found in the print shop. They were in the Writing Department, in the administration, and in congregations all around New York. We were shocked at how deep his tentacles had spread, how many of our esteemed leaders had participated in the apostate conspiracies. We listened to tape recordings, we saw photographs of secret meetings and lists of dubious literature discovered in the rooms of the disfellowshipped leaders.

Vic Raymond's excommunication led to a reorganization of the Writing Department. Miller was given more responsibilities, and thus I also got new tasks.

My responsibilities were now more connected to the application development of MEPS than to the actual printing process. Miller knew that I could write, and from time to time I got writing assignments. Mostly it was about editing something somebody else wrote. Once or twice I wrote an article from start to finish. Miller had it printed as his own. We never stated author's names; everybody just had a desk code. I, of course, had no desk code—I was a foreign intern and wasn't supposed to write articles. Therefore, all of my texts were recorded under Miller's code.

Ron Miller was busy during this time, and we didn't meet face to face that often. Sometimes I saw him in the C-wing, and he always greeted me but had no time to talk.

But on this warm morning, there was a note on my desk saying that Miller wanted to see me.

"How do you feel about Nebraska?" he asked me when I sat down. He often cut to the chase without typical American small talk.

What did I feel about Nebraska? It sounded like a trick question in school when the teacher asked something and the most important thing was to try to guess what the teacher thought was the correct answer. I assumed the question was rhetorical so I raised my eyebrows to show that I didn't know how I felt about Nebraska.

"We have kept an eye on you," Miller said. He made the word "we" sound as if it included not only Miller and one or two other brothers, but the whole floor or possibly the entire headquarters.

"We need brothers like you, who can express themselves in speech and writing. You have managed to keep out of the internal power fights, and that is an advantage these days."

I knew what he meant. Some of Vic Raymond's supporters couldn't be charged with anything specific, but those brothers and sisters had seen their assignments and privileges withdrawn. Many of them quietly disappeared from the headquarters to their own congregations far away. Others stayed, but they had become like ghosts, avoiding eye contact when I met them in the corridors.

"It's possible that one day you will be working on the eighth floor. Who knows, maybe even on the ninth. It's important that you gain practical experience of leading a congregation. You would start as a pioneer and a ministerial servant, then a few years later you may become an elder. Everything is possible. I think you have a unique talent and you being from Europe is no disadvantage at all—on the contrary, there has been pressure to open up positions to non-Americans. A few years of hands-on experience in various congregations, then back to Brooklyn."

I chose not to comment.

"There's an opening in McCook, Nebraska."

It sounded as if there was a vacant position that you could apply for by filling in an application.

*

"Where in the hell is McCook, Nebraska?" Alison said that night. We opened the *Reader's Digest Atlas of the World* and found McCook close to the border between Nebraska and Kansas, hundreds of miles from the nearest big city.

There was only one congregation in McCook, and the growth potential was great, according to Miller. I would be assigned to McCook for four or five years as a ministerial servant with administrative tasks.

"So now you're going to rise through the ranks in the organization," Alison said. "You'll be one of those high officials who walk with their lackeys in tow and make decisions about other people's lives."

"Firstly, I will become a ministerial servant. It's a far cry from making any decisions. Secondly, your idea of leadership is pretty odd."

"I'm not so sure about that. One time when there was an assembly in Syracuse, some big shot from Brooklyn visited our circuit. You should have seen the submissive buttering up. Every time somebody comes from Brooklyn, it's the same thing. The brothers didn't know how to be courteous and accommodating enough. And the sisters were after them as if they were rock stars. Nobody literally threw their panties on stage, of course, but some of the old busters took advantage of the situation."

"I find that hard to believe."

"Markus, you are starry-eyed. When men achieve a certain position, they think they can do anything. That they are entitled. You must have heard about the wife-swapping scandal in Halcyon. There is a certain house in Brooklyn where things happen."

"But they were disfellowshipped."

"Not all of them. Some they wanted to get rid of. Others belonged to the inner circle."

She thought about it for a moment.

"Besides, we should be disfellowshipped too. We follow our own rules."

She was right.

I couldn't fully explain why our love felt justified and beautiful when according to our rules it was dirty and forbidden. But Alison was right. I also felt I had the right to disobey rules. I lived in the fuzzy zone defined by the truth and what was left unsaid, by what the rules stipulated and what my conscience allowed me to do.

We had been circumspect, and we never appeared together in places where anyone could recognize us. Alison usually attended our assembly, and I attended theirs. But we only appeared temporarily together; we never held hands, we didn't take the same route home, or even leave at the same time. That was particularly important to Alison; she had to be cautious due to her past. I had a little more wiggle room because I was a man, a foreigner, and I worked at the headquarters.

When I informed Miller that I was willing to move to Nebraska, he called me to his office again. He had a troubled wrinkle on his forehead.

"We have recently learned that you like to spend time with Alison Killarney," he said.

This was one of those moments in life when you know that something is about to happen, something that can change everything, and then you realize that everything has already changed and that you have known it all along. I felt a strange quiver, as if I had stepped on a loose stone that shifted in an unexpected direction under my weight.

The seconds stretched with the elasticity of a rubber band.

Miller flipped through a folder as if it were full of information about Alison and me. I wasn't surprised that they knew, because it was impossible to keep such things secret. The relevant question was how much they knew.

"Of course, we don't want to dictate your choices, but I'm sure you are aware of the Biblical principles that apply. May I assume that your relationship is pure?"

I decided to understand the questions literally. I nodded. It was a good idea to assume that.

"I couldn't imagine anything else. But there is something that you should know. Nothing wrong with Alison Killarney. On the contrary, she is a theocratic girl. Last August she worked as an auxiliary pioneer, and she reported no less than 100 hours. And she's attractive, if you are into that Irish type of women. But there is this one thing you should know about. A few years ago she was almost disfellowshipped. I won't go into details, but let's say that things happened that shouldn't happen before marriage. Sister Killarney showed remorse during the hearing, and she didn't attempt to deny or downplay her actions. She wasn't disfellowshipped, but she lost her privileges, of course. After that, her behavior has been impeccable."

He pretended to consult his papers.

"You have been seen together. Do you have plans to marry?"

My visa was about to expire, and I didn't have a work permit. I wasn't sure what Miller was getting at, so I chose my words carefully.

"We intend to move forward slowly."

"Excellent. On the one hand, the apostle Paul says that it's better to marry than to burn with desire, but on the other hand, this is something you should consider prudently. I won't mention any names, but the brother she committed sin with works here at the headquarters now. Would you be able to live with the thought that your wife has been a public toilet, that her hands have touched a man who may be your overseer or somebody you supervise? How would it feel to know that he has taken her virginity, that he has seen her naked, that he has squeezed her breasts? I hope you understand."

I said nothing. He looked into my eyes and nodded slowly.

"I hope you understand," he said again.

I understood.

Alison had cooked a lamb stew and opened a bottle of California red wine. She had set the table with a white tablecloth and candles.

Before we began to eat, she gave me a package.

"It's nothing really, just a joke."

It was a white t-shirt with text on it: *Where in the hell is McCook, Nebraska?*

"You should wear it for breakfast at the office. Miller and the others would choke on their morning coffee."

I smiled. The gift was typical of Alison: funny, but useless.

I tasted the wine and poured some into Alison's glass too, but she didn't drink it. She lit the candles and carried the stew pot in. She closed the door to the fridge with her foot and simultaneously put out the ceiling lamp with her elbow in a single comfortable movement.

"Did Miller say anything about when?" she asked as we were eating.

"Within a month, I think. The need is great."

"One month? That means we have to marry soon. There is no time for planning."

I didn't respond to that, and she sank into a troubled silence.

"But that's all right," she said. "I don't care about a princess wedding."

I looked up, and she chose to misunderstand my expression.

"I mean it. I don't care. Of course, a big wedding would be nice, but that's not possible now."

"No," I said and shuffled pieces of meat on my plate. "That's not possible now."

A couple of times during the evening Alison asked if everything was all right and I said yes. I felt her eyes on my back when I did the dishes.

We watched *The Tonight Show* together, but I had trouble focusing.

I was afraid that I might not be able to man up for the night, but it went well. Our union was silent and almost unbearably slow, without passion but with lots of tenderness. It ended with a warm wave rather than fireworks. I was still hard, and we lay for a long time in each other's arms.

Did I say something? Possibly. An attempt at an explanation, an excusing gesture. If I did say something, I said it with such a soft voice that she couldn't hear it. Or maybe she heard what I didn't say.

I think I heard her cry during the night.

When she got up to go to work, I pretended to sleep. She clanked a little with her coffee cup and the plate as if she wanted to wake me up and for a moment I was aware that she was standing by the bed looking at me. I only had to extend my arm, and she would have crawled back to bed and followed me all the way to, say, Alaska. But that was not possible. Miller had said what he said, and I was in no position to question him.

I heard Alison write something on a piece of paper and then she left.

I gathered all my small accessories, my toothbrush, my shaving kit, a couple of paperbacks. I left her key on the table.

.

15

Jazz was a short-lived fascination for Ellen. She bought one single jazz album, *Night and Day* by Django Reinhardt and Stéphane Grappelli. She played it time and again on our Dux. She listened intently, her eyes fixed on the turntable needle as if it could give her information in addition to what the built-in speakers produced. Then she lifted the needle and played the tune from memory on the violin; she mimicked the idioms and the phrases. As she became more skilled she played along, adding her own jazz tune as a counterpoint, or—and this I never heard anybody else do, this was her own invention—she played a baroque voice over the wild jazz, a voice that could have been written by Bach or Händel. This was of course based on her knowledge of the key and the chord progression, but to us who listened, it sounded as if Bach and Django Reinhardt had composed a piece together, a piece with two different meanings, depending on how you listened. Like one of those optical illusions where you can see either a duck or a rabbit in the same image, two faces or a vase.

Her interest in jazz started on a wet winter day when she was eight and I was eleven. I still played the piano at the time, but not particularly well. I liked to listen and analyze, but my ambitions never extended beyond Aaron's and Thompson's piano books. I could identify quality music, but could not produce it myself.

It was Carola's turn to get Sofia from daycare, so I took Ellen to her music lesson. Ellen had music lessons five days a week, three violin lessons, one music theory lesson, and an afternoon with the orchestra. Her violin lessons and the theory lesson took place in Herttoniemi, but the orchestra rehearsal was at the Conservatory on Fredrikinkatu Street. Ellen had no sense of direction, and she had trouble remembering which bus she was supposed to take and where she was going and she quickly got lost if she absentmindedly walked a block or two in the wrong direction. Mother couldn't keep track of all her lessons, so it became Carola's responsibility and mine to make sure Ellen was in the right place at the right time.

It was snowing when we left for the orchestra rehearsal. The temperature was just above freezing, and the snow melted as soon as it hit the ground. We took the bus downtown and stopped outside the Stockmann department store to look at the Christmas windows. We shouldn't have done that; Christmas was a pagan festival, but Ellen was eight, and she loved the gewgaw and the Christmas lights. She gazed at the automatic goblins and at the electric trains that went around and around, at the skating tracks made of mirrors, at the straw goats. Her eyes shone.

The orchestra rehearsal would soon begin, so we had to hurry on. We passed by the Stockmann main entrance and proceeded to Mannerheimintie Street. Ellen had her violin case on her back, and she skipped, the little girl that she was, straight into the puddles in the dirty snow. Then she remembered that she was supposed to walk properly when she carried her violin, and she gave me an anxious look. I didn't scold her. She smiled a coquettish smile when she realized that she'd gotten away with it this time.

I took her hand, and we waited together for the green light at the zebra crossing. An elderly lady smiled at her.

"Such a sweet little girl," she said to me.

Ellen beamed at the woman.

"I'm growing up to become a really charming young lady," she said.

We were already late when we arrived at the Conservatory. The elevator was out of order, so we ran up the stairs. On each floor, you could hear a cacophony of various instruments and different types of music behind the closed doors.

The smaller concert hall was on the third floor and, the doors open, we could hear an ensemble playing. What we heard sounded so strange and alluring that Ellen and I stopped and looked at each other. Without a word, we tiptoed to the door.

A jazz quartet was playing. I knew the music, it was "Autumn Leaves," an odd choice considering the season. I wasn't sure how I knew what they were playing because it was as if the saxophone just wriggled around the melody and played all possible notes except for the right ones. But I was sure, it was the same "Autumn Leaves" that Mantovani's Orchestra played on the record we had at home.

This version was different. The time signature, a traditional 4/4, was the same as in the original, but the structure of the piece seemed stretched out and chopped into pieces. The melody was implied, but it was harmonized with peculiar chords. It sounded as if the bass and the chord weren't in the same key. Everything was oddly warped but in a deliberate way.

The bass walked up and down the scale and made random dance moves as if to catch up with the piano's syncopated rhythm. The saxophone had its quirks and climbed and twisted around the harmonies. The drummer seemed to know when the saxophonist would breathe and added a couple of hits to fill the space.

I didn't know if they invented everything as they played or if the whole thing was rehearsed. I heard a short quote from another piece of music I knew but didn't remember its name. It seemed as if the saxophonist leaped out through a hole in the music and enjoyed a moment of freedom outside, only to get pulled back into the rest of the group that had gleefully allowed the saxophone a brief extra-musical affair.

Then something happened, as if the musicians had agreed in advance to play with the audience's expectations. The melody became strangely skewed, the musical key shifting at the same time the pianist started playing triplets without increasing the tempo. The effect was that the music seemed to go slower, as if it zoomed in on the remaining notes. Then the saxophone soared up in the stratosphere, made some rapid chromatic runs at the upper limit of the instrument's range, and then tumbled down like an autumn leaf back to the key-note and died out in a soft whisper.

We had eavesdropped to the quartet far too long; we were late to the lesson. We ran up to the fourth floor and gently opened the door to the big rehearsal room so as not to disturb. The rehearsal was in full swing. They rehearsed a string arrangement of Schubert's "Ave Maria." When László Király spotted us, he knocked on the music stand until the music stopped.

He directed his words both to Ellen and to me.

"This is an orchestra rehearsal, not a—" He searched for the right word, "not a *kindergarten*. We start on time. We show each other respect. We are an ensemble, we do not come and go as we please."

Ellen looked down and took her place.

"Ellen. You are the most gifted student I've ever had. You'll become somebody one day. But not like this. Big girl. You should know better."

Ellen's bottom lip trembled. László Király scowled at her. He laid his hand on her shoulder.

Ellen froze and opened her eyes wide.

"Don't touch me. I'm extremely sensitive."

László Király was so stunned that he blinked.

When we got home, Ellen showed me the piano score to "Ave Maria."

"Accompany me," she commanded.

I hesitated. Both Ellen and I knew that "Ave Maria" was church music, and Catholic to boot, so it was definitely not allowed at home.

I studied the score and tried the accompaniment on the piano. I wasn't good at playing prima vista, but this piece wasn't that difficult. I let my fingers glide over the keys, and the magic from the notes was transferred through my hands to the piano keys and to the strings that vibrated and filled the room with tones. Occasionally I stumbled, but I kept the rhythm and Ellen improvised over the chord changes. Her playing was jazzy, a bit clumsy and unrecognizable, but she had an intuitive feel for how the jazz syntax worked, and she remembered a few phrases by heart.

We were so focused on our playing that we didn't hear Father come home. Suddenly he was standing behind us, frowning.

"What kind of music is that?"

I couldn't lie, but neither did I want to admit that we had spent time playing Catholic music. I felt the panic grow — how much had he heard? The accompaniment itself was simply consecutive thirds and fourths in a predictable rhythm. What Ellen played bore no resemblance to the original melody. But the chord changes were so readily identifiable that Mother would have been able to name the music based on the first bar. But Father, luckily, wasn't musically gifted. He was just suspicious.

That's when I realized something about the truth and about leaving things unsaid. It was Father's own fault that he didn't know music history. I didn't have to lie, I just told the truth.

"It's a song by Schubert, from 1825, to a text by Walter Scott. But in German of course."

"I like Schubert. What's the name of the song?"

"It's Opus 52, number 6. The name of the song is 'Ellens dritter gesang.'"

"Ellen's third song," Father muttered and shook his head to show that he had never heard of that song.

There is no need to tell the whole truth to those who don't need to know it. You can hide the truth without lying, you can break the rules by following them.

Part III

Debra

BEN KALLAND

16

Before I moved to McCook, I had lived near water my entire life. The summers I spent at Bellevue, the winters in Helsinki. In Brooklyn, the sea, or at least the river, was always there. I used to think that a city should have bridges and water, that the topography, the seashore, the bays and the islands defined the boundaries of the city. But McCook was situated in the middle of the prairie. They told me that the town had grown around the train station, but I thought that the relationship between cause and effect was unclear.

The Nebraska summers were hot; sometimes you could see a tornado. In the fall it could be seventy degrees one day, and freezing the next morning. The winters were cold and snowy. When it snowed, we sometimes got twelve inches in one go, and the blizzards lasted for days.

The highlight of the year was hunting grouse with Chris Huebinger. I didn't care much for the hunting per se, but I enjoyed spending time outdoors. I liked the open landscape and the frosty autumn mornings, and I liked Chris' company. He too was a ministerial servant in the congregation, and we quickly became good friends. He was a year younger than I was, but when I moved to McCook, he already had a family — a wife and a two-month-old baby. Chris assisted me with practical arrangements, finding a place to live, a job, buying a car. He taught me how to interpret the grumpy but friendly ways of the Midwesterners.

During my first years in McCook, I lived on the outskirts of the town, on the second floor of a small house. The rent was cheap, and although the room was small, it was good enough for me. There were no jobs in the printing industry in McCook, but Brother Jablonsky hired me to work in his cleaning firm, and I earned enough to pay the rent and the car loan. In New York, I didn't need a car, but on the prairies of Nebraska, it was indispensable.

My first tasks in the new congregation were of an administrative nature. The congregation was disorganized, at least by Brooklyn standards. There were no territory cards; field service was performed unsystematically and randomly. I introduced the good practices I had learned in the Farragut congregation. I divided McCook into one hundred territories, drew the boundaries on a map with a red marker, cut out every territory and glued it on a piece of cardboard. I numbered the territories and made a list of them, and now the publishers could take a card, cover the area in a couple of weeks or a month, and make notes about who lived there and how they accepted the truth. Chris Huebinger made sure every territory was covered at least once a year. The congregation welcomed my method with astonishing enthusiasm; they thought the technique was fabulous.

Sofia married at the age of nineteen to Arto Tanner, who was ten years her senior and an elder in a congregation in Turku.

I would have liked to attend the wedding, but I couldn't due to my visa problem. I didn't think of myself as an illegal immigrant—that was a term used for Mexican housekeepers. But my tourist visa wasn't valid anymore. For some time, there had been rumors of a new law, the Immigration Control and Reform Act, which would force employers to verify the work permits of all employees. The law also applied to my organization, but on the other hand, the same law promised a permanent residence permit to any immigrant who had been living in the country continuously for five years. I had been living in the US for four years, so I didn't want to take the risk. I sent Sofia a telegram.

In exchange, I got their wedding photo. Sofia also asked about Bellevue. After Timo Auramo's drowning accident, the cottage had been rented to outsiders, but now Sofia suggested she and her husband could use Bellevue as a summer residence. Arto Tanner was an electrician by profession and instead of paying rent, he could refurbish and wire the cottage for electricity.

I called Carola, who had moved back to Helsinki to study at the university.

"I tried to call Sofia once," she said. "She hung up on me without a word. So I don't really feel like doing her any favors. But on the other hand, I have no use for Bellevue myself, so I don't mind if she and her husband start using the cottage."

When Debra Haas moved to McCook the next spring, I initially didn't feel attracted to her. But she was the kind of woman whom most people either considered attractive or assumed everybody else considered attractive.

Debra was a fearless, big woman with a shrill and rippling laugh. She was born into a Midwestern working-class family, but her appearance was more like what they called a California blonde—hair like that in a shampoo commercial and flashing white teeth. The type of woman you can find in the reception area of a gym or on the cover of car magazines, leaning over the bonnet of a V8.

The congregation in McCook had a female majority, like all other congregations, and there were not many unmarried young men. I was a ministerial servant and had been working at the headquarters. Therefore I was popular with the young women and especially with their mothers. And being a foreigner was no disadvantage. When Debra moved to McCook, some of the sisters disapproved of her and considered her a competitor and a migrating bird. That was the expression used for sisters who moved from one congregation to another in search of a husband. If no suitable candidate appeared, they would move to another congregation after six or twelve months.

Even though I wasn't that interested in the beginning, many others thought we would be a good fit. When Debra became a full-time pioneer, the congregation overseer, Brother Jablonsky, praised her deep spirituality.

"Sister Debra Haas is theocratic and chaste and from a respectable family. Her father is an elder. She's in your league."

Debra and I often found ourselves in the same field service group or the same cleaning group or the same volunteer group during assemblies. We sat together during meetings.

In the beginning, our relationship was just innocent flirting. When it became more serious, we sometimes drove outside the town, often over the border to Kansas, where nobody knew us.

In August, Chris Huebinger and I were appointed elders. It was a stripped-down event, just a short announcement from the stage. Before that, I had received the Flock book, the secret book for elders, a book no ordinary publishers were allowed to read.

Brother Jablonsky handed it solemnly to me. It wasn't even a book, it was a bunch of papers stapled together.

"You have to keep this locked in a drawer at all times. You may laminate it or have it spiral bound, but you have to do it yourself or have another elder do it. If a brother who is not an elder does it for you, then you must watch while the work is being done. You must not let a sister do it, let alone an unbeliever."

Chris Huebinger and I perused the Flock book together. The content proved to be a disappointment as it was mostly dull instructions about administrative procedures. The interesting parts were the detailed instructions about judicial committees and disfellowshipping and about approved and disapproved sexual conduct.

Debra and I had been dating for six months when she suggested that we visit her parents to help them move a piano.

It was a chilly Saturday morning in the middle of November. Debra's parents lived in Kearney, a couple of hours drive from McCook. The town was considerably larger than McCook; it even had a university, but it was still a town. The US 30 ran through it and had we continued, we would have been outside the town in a couple of minutes.

When I parked the car in the driveway in front of a house that resembled a shoe box, Debra's father was standing on the porch. He looked ex-military, straight back and buzz cut.

"They don't make cars like that anymore," he said studying my car.

I nodded thoughtfully. I didn't know if he meant that everything used to be better or that this particular model wasn't in production anymore.

Debra's mother was considerably younger than her husband, and to my surprise, she was small and slender, not like her daughter at all.

Debra's half-sister Leah, in her forties, and her grandmother were there too. It was clear that this was an interview of a potential son-in-law.

It was difficult to move the piano because they had no carrying straps, but after an hour's worth of huffing and puffing, Leah's husband, Debra's father, and I had moved it to its new place in the basement. I tried a few chords to test that the tuning hadn't been affected.

"Do you play the piano?" Debra seemed genuinely surprised, as if I had deliberately misled her in that respect.

In the afternoon we prepared for the barbecue. All the while I felt as if I had an employment interview. They asked questions about Finland, about my future plans, about Brooklyn. Debra chimed in by asking penetrating follow-up questions.

Her father was a typical American elder who maintained order in his family and probably was thinking that if it hadn't been for some unfortunate coincidences and the elbows of b higher in the organization. By profession, he was a maintenance man for the local electrical company, but he was already retired. He lectured me on how importing cars had cut jobs in Detroit and how the sheet metal Japanese car manufacturers used was so thin that it almost was paper.

We talked about inflation, the president's authority, about the difficulties the farmers were facing, and about the corruption in Washington. I agreed with everything he said, and after a while, I realized that this annoyed him. To find something we could disagree on, he brought up the current debate about capital punishment in Nebraska. It hadn't been used for decades.

"You Europeans," he said, "you are so weak on this question. You think that somebody who has broken the law is flawed in some respect and should be repaired. You Europeans think we should pamper the criminals and correct them and return them to society. But a man isn't a machine. Man is created to be God's image. A man has a free choice and is able to distinguish right from wrong. He has responsibility for his actions. All actions have a price, the more serious the action, the higher the price. Doesn't the Bible give examples of actions that deserve death?"

I admitted that there were actions that could only be reconciled by death. Debra's father snorted.

When we lit the barbecue, we realized that we were out of barbecue sauce. I volunteered to drive to Wal-Mart to get whatever was missing, and Debra quickly volunteered to come along.

We only drove for a couple of minutes before we had to stop. The road to the shopping center was closed. There had been an accident in the intersection, apparently recently. The emergency vehicles were still there.

We got out of the car and joined the group of people standing at the site of the accident. There was an uncanny silence. The traffic stood still, the spectators watched the drama without talking. The paramedics administered first aid to a bloody victim still trapped inside the vehicle. In the silence, it was easy to imagine the sound that ensued when the cars came to a screaming halt and metal wrinkled and glass shattered all over the intersection.

Debra pressed against me. It was chilly, and she was trembling. We said nothing during the whole time the paramedics tried to resuscitate the victim. It was dramatic but soothing at the same time. Once more, somebody else was the victim.

Somebody pulled a piece of black cloth over the head of the victim and Debra started crying. I comforted and hugged her. I thought about Ellen. How people must have watched, glutting in evil and sudden death. How her life had ended in a fraction of a second, how she barely had realized what was about to happen.

Finally, a tow truck arrived and moved the wrecked cars to the side. We returned to the car. The line of cars crept between the pavement and the wreckage.

After a couple of blocks, Debra knocked on the side window to make me turn. She steered me toward the reservoir and then to a side street close to the park. I parked under a couple of low-hanging branches. I let the engine run to keep the car warm.

For a while we just sat there in silence, looking forward. Debra took my hand and put her head on my shoulder. We kissed.

"We don't have much time," she said and glanced around. Nobody was there. The trees hid the car, and the parking space was empty.

I think I was turned on by the close encounter with sudden death. Debra was perhaps turned on by the thought that her parents believed we were shopping.

I felt her breasts through the jacket. I suggested that we move to the back seat, but she peeked at her watch and lowered her head into my lap.

I forgot about evil and sudden death. I forgot it was cold outside. I touched her face with the tips of my fingers. Her lips were soft and warm.

I closed my eyes.

I was thinking of another woman. I remembered how she slept naked on top of the sheets one hot summer night. I remembered how her lips had tasted of coffee in the morning.

When I was close, I tapped Debra on the top of her head, as was our habit, but she continued.

Alison.

Debra froze. Only when she lifted her head and hit me in the face with her open hand, I realized that I had said it aloud.

I also realized that it would have been meaningless to try and explain, I could only make it worse.

She screamed, shut the car door with a bang and ran down the street toward the center of the town.

We kept our appearances up the rest of the evening. Debra was exaggeratedly polite, and I played the gentleman.

She slept in the car while we drove back to McCook. I felt remorseful but a bit relieved at the same time. I already imagined how we would have a serious conversation, and I would be calm and dispassionate, and she would be a bit hysterical in the beginning, and it would end with us going our separate ways, but we would promise to still be friends.

I misjudged her completely.

*

We met at a café the next day. I chose a public place because I wanted to avoid a scene.

"We have done wrong, we have to confess to the brothers," Debra said.

I hadn't been expecting that.

"Are you crazy? Why would we tell anyone?"

"Because it's unclean."

"It's nobody's business."

She didn't reply but looked out of the window. It had snowed the night before. The snow wouldn't stay for long, but at the moment the town appeared clean, placid, and curiously sleepy.

I was sure Debra was bluffing, but I didn't understand what she was trying to do.

"Do what you want, but I will be no part of it."

She eyed me as if I was a harmless but vaguely disgusting insect and a rather small and colorless specimen at that.

"You know how it works: I'm going to confess. If you don't, it means that you are not repenting and you'll be disfellowshipped."

She was serious.

"Debbie. Honey. Why would we do ourselves a disservice?"

She finished her coffee and got up.

"Today, before the meeting."

Debra had made her decision, and I had no choice. We told the overseer that we had unfortunate and rather serious news.

The next day we appeared before the judicial committee.

Brother Jablonsky was the chairman of the three brothers in the committee. They seemed uncomfortable.

"It's disappointing to hear this. Not that we don't understand, we have been young too, but that's no excuse. On the other hand, it's encouraging that you bring this up yourselves."

They read an excerpt from the magazine that covered immorality and loose conduct, then they prayed and read some Bible verses aloud. Debra and I answered their questions in shame and assured them that we hadn't been guilty of fornication, just of unclean conduct. Debra cried a little.

We waited outside the library room of the congregation while the committee deliberated. We didn't look at each other.

They called us in. They read one more verse from the Bible and another excerpt from the magazine and concluded that our lapse was serious. But since we had confessed uncompelled, it wasn't worth making a big deal of it.

"But there is one condition," Brother Jablonsky said. "You have to get married as soon as possible."

I glanced at Debra. I could see a glint in her eye, a content, self-congratulatory expression as if she thought that she not only got away with it but had actually reached her goal.

One week later we drove in complete silence to Denver and took a flight to Las Vegas.

It had proved impossible to marry quickly in Nebraska. But it was possible in Nevada. Debra was sulking. She had wanted to plan decorations and catering, she had wanted a fancy bridal gown and a string quartet and two hundred guests. She didn't say a word to me during the whole trip.

Debra's parents and Chris Huebinger and his wife traveled with us; they would be wedding witnesses. Debra's father had booked a non-religious marriage ceremony in an all-night wedding chapel.

There are moments in life that only take a second, but contain years. I have heard that when your life is in danger, you can see your life in a compressed cavalcade.

I listened to the monotone voice that probably had uttered the same litany ten times that day. I didn't see my whole life in front of me, only a few short moments, sharply rendered.

I saw Ellen playing on the cliff, I saw Carola pack her tiny suitcase one early morning. I saw Alison in her summer dress outside the assembly hall. I asked her if she wanted something to drink, and she said:

"I do."

We took the wedding picture in an adjacent room. Afterward, we had dinner at an all-you-can-eat buffet. Debra and her mother picked at the food, but Chris Huebinger made sure he got his money's worth. He loaded plate after plate with potato salad and pork ribs.

Debra's father had paid for a superior room on the eighth floor of the Dunes hotel. We had a view of the boulevard and the well-lit casinos. On the king-size bed lay a bouquet of flowers and a towel folded into a swan, and on the side table was a metal bucket with champagne on ice.

Debra locked herself in the bathroom while I opened the bottle and filled the glasses. When she came out, she was wearing a thick flannel nightgown. I got up, but she writhed by me without even looking at me.

"Don't try anything. I mean it."

She sat down on the bed and brushed her hair with long strokes. I joined her. I thought of something to say and put my hand on hers.

"If you touch me, I'll scream."

I smiled at her like I used to smile at Ellen when she made a fuss because the boots were the wrong color. I stretched my arms out to hug her.

Debra opened her mouth and inhaled loudly. It was apparent that she didn't give a thought to the thin walls—or maybe she was actually considering them.

"Okay," I said and retracted my hands with the palms toward her. "Okay."

She pulled the bedsheet up and turned her reading light off.

I lay motionless, listening. Debra's parents were in the adjacent room. When I listened carefully, I could hear a soft mumble from their television. The air-conditioning unit hummed. From the window, I could hear the quiet noise of the traffic outside.

When Debra's breathing became regular, I got up and pulled the shades. In principle the view was magnificent because you could see all over Las Vegas, but what you saw was just the neon lights, reflected in the swimming pools and fountains of the neighboring hotels.

I knew how everything would look in the sharpness of the morning light. The yellowish walls that now seemed cozy would appear dirty. There would be undefined stains on the carpet, and the champagne would prove to be a cheap, semi-sweet American sparkling wine. The merciless sun would reveal that behind the skyscrapers and billboards sprawled a desert.

I considered calling Carola.

I went back to the bed and started rocking the mattress, at first slowly, then faster and with more pressure as the momentum began to build. Debra woke up, sat halfway up and turned toward me. I rocked the bed faster so that it screeched and creaked. The bed moved an inch, and the legs scraped against the wall-to-wall carpet. Debra's eyes widened; she was unable to understand what I was doing. I stared her in the eyes and rocked the bed so much that the headboard hit the wall. I moaned a couple of times dramatically and continued the pounding until her face crinkled into a grimace and she got up and ran, sobbing, to the bathroom.

Then I stopped.

Illogically and inexplicably, I felt free.

17

In addition to taking care of practical things like making sure that Ellen got food and went to her music lessons on time, we taught her how to navigate life. How to answer stupid questions by classmates: Why don't you celebrate Christmas, don't you believe in Jesus, are you allowed to watch television, do you have a front-loading washing machine, do you have a dozen siblings, are you allowed to drink Coca-Cola? How to pretend not to hear when your parents argued, how you could make yourself invisible when needed, how to avoid overly friendly men who looked at you like a predator fish at something shiny and fast-moving.

Carola and I grew quickly. We were clumsy; my voice deepened, Carola's body softened. Ellen was still a child, and Sofia hadn't gone to school yet. Timo was already a young man.

It was a hot day, in the middle of one of those extended high pressures that seemed to fill our childhood summers. It was too early in the summer to pick bilberries and too hot to run around, so we just sat on the sunny cliffs and looked down at the sea.

We couldn't see our cottage, nor Timo's, because the shore made an inward bend right below us. It felt like we were on a deserted island. The rocky coast between the pilot station and our cottage was uninhabited, no houses, no roads, few natural harbors. You couldn't discern any buildings on Upinniemi either, because the distance was too far, and the cottages were built a bit from the shore. The only signs of life were a couple of sailing boats on the horizon and a pair of eider ducks swimming below us.

Timo tossed a stone around in his hand.

"Let's see who can hit those eiders," he suggested.

"Those are no eiders," Carola said.

Now we could see it too. What we had thought were eiders were, in fact, a couple of heads bobbing in a natural sea pool, inside a wave breaker formed from underwater rocks. We saw bundles of clothes and a bag on the shore. We had no idea who they were. They hadn't arrived by boat, so they must have walked along the shore, hoping to find a secluded place.

They got out of the water, a young couple. It looked so serene and Eden-like when they sat down on the warm rocks, naked, drying themselves in the sun. After a while, they got up and spread their towels. Their bodies left wet marks that resembled psychological inkblot tests on the rock. The man kissed the woman and put a hand on her breast. A moment later he was on top of her, and it looked like they were wrestling. Timo, Carola, and I glanced at each other. We got up, but Ellen didn't want to go.

"What are they doing?" she asked.

"It's some game," I said.

"What kind of game?"

I didn't feel like coming up with something, so I shrugged.

"I think they are copulating," Ellen said.

Timo suppressed a laugh.

"Do you even know what that means?"

ELLEN'S SONG

"It's the same thing as fucking," she said and took my hand. "But I'm too young to know things like that."

I decided to give her a lecture. I told her how men and women are built differently and how babies are made. The description was vague but basically correct.

She rolled her eyes.

"I knew that. I'm a child, I'm not stupid. But why do they want to make a baby right now?"

"You see, when a man and a woman love each other, they sometimes do that just for fun."

"Really?" Ellen's pupils dilated like a drop of watercolor in a glass. "Why?"

I didn't know what to say. Timo helped me out.

"Because it feels wonderful. Everybody does it."

Ellen stared at us, then at the couple down there. You could see that she was trying to process the new information. She always looked like that when she searched inside and tried to figure things out.

"Are you ever going to do that?" she finally said. "I'm not going to. Ever."

Timo, Carola, and I secretly smiled.

"It's so depraved," Ellen added when she saw our smiles and understood that there was something she didn't know about.

Then something occurred to her, something she had heard during a meeting.

"Unless, of course, I get married. When a man and a woman are united in matrimony, they will become one flesh. Then they will be able to enjoy their relation fully, without the unwanted and sometimes disastrous consequences of premarital relations."

145

*

Timo Auramo was the one who taught me about sex.

"Do you know what it feels like to touch a breast?" he asked once. I was thirteen, he was sixteen.

I had never thought about what that would feel like.

"A breast is soft and firm at the same time," he beamed proudly.

During the weekend he had had his hand inside the shirt of a certain Jaana Kajander and, according to him, inside her pants too. Now he gave a detailed account of how it had felt.

I wasn't sure about how I was expected to react. To play ignorant would have made me look childish, but nodding supportively would have implied that I had done something similar myself. I put on the demeanor Father usually put on when Ellen and I discussed a complicated musical term, like counterpoint—an expression that implied that he had heard about it but wasn't particularly interested.

Even though Timo Auramo probably was exaggerating, he had sinned and could be disfellowshipped. I wondered how he had dared to do it. I dreaded the possibility that I would do something like that, would get caught and be forced to explain to the elders where my hands had been.

Timo had shown me his brothers' secret magazines, but there was nothing new in them, I had seen women and girls swimming in the sea after the sauna or sunbathing on the rocky shore. I knew there were big and small breasts, pointed and puffy, pear-shaped and apple-shaped. Some were white, some tanned. I was an expert on breasts without understanding them at all.

But that spring, I learned that what you can't see might be more interesting than what is on display. Strangely enough,

Timo didn't teach me that; I learned it all by myself during a matinee in the music institute.

Carola and I performed a four-handed version of Sinding's *Frühlingsrauschen*, a piece that sounds impressive because there are numerous fast runs. In fact, it's rather easy for a couple of thirteen-year-olds. Ellen played the *Carmen Fantasy* by Sarasate.

That concert was Ellen's first major accomplishment. Her piece was the final performance of the concert and its virtuoso culmination. The *Carmen Fantasy* is a piece you play to show off. All possible playing techniques are employed: spiccato, harmonics, double stops. Ellen and the pianist tossed the piece between them as if they were playing badminton. Toward the end, when the tempo was at its peak, Ellen's small hand jumped between the first and the seventh position, and she stretched her little finger to reach the highest notes and then she finished the piece exactly at the same moment as the pianist.

When the thunder of applause started, we realized how other people perceived her. To them, she wasn't our kid sister, she was a talent, a promising star.

I, however, remember the concert best because of Ellen's accompanist, a piano teacher. She didn't wear a bra, as was the fashion at that time. Or at least it seemed that way if you looked carefully. Most of the male students, and probably her colleagues, did look carefully. She wore a silk blouse, dark blue, almost black. During the concert, she went to the stage several times to accompany some reluctant little soloist, and every time, she had to pass the large window where the spring sun streamed in. The blouse became practically transparent against the light. We didn't need much imagination to make out how her foxy breasts moved under the silk blouse. There were silent gasps and rustles of fabric when elbows poked into neighbors.

Suddenly I became aware of women. They had been there all the time, but I had never really seen them. Now they were everywhere, and I observed them in awe as if I just had learned that they were aliens from outer space.

Timo Auramo's stories became interesting, albeit a bit filthy, and they fed my imagination. Many nights I mentally pawed Jaana Kajander's breasts, even though I didn't even know who she was.

I also found interesting books. The initial reason I borrowed books written by Henry Miller was that the name was almost identical to Ronald Henry Miller's. The librarian knew me and recommended interesting books, but she hesitated when I wanted to borrow *Quiet Days in Clichy*.

"We have lots of new young adult books too," she said. She seemed to be having an internal struggle. "You can take it, but take this one too." She put *The Outsider* on top of the heap.

It was sort of a package deal, and I accepted it because I liked to read Camus too.

I got tired of writing ghost stories and started writing adventure stories instead. Mostly they were about airplanes, bandits, and foreign countries, but sometimes the story got sidetracked into Henry Miller territory.

"You shouldn't read that kind of books," Ellen said as she studied the woman on the cover of one of Miller's books. "They are inappropriate for boys your age."

I took her head under my arm and rubbed her scalp until she screamed and wriggled free.

"Ellen, you are impossible."

"I'm not impossible. This is just a phase. I will get over it when I grow older."

We were teenagers, not children anymore. Our hormones ran amok and obscured our judgment and caused our brains to make connections that only a teenager can make. During the meetings, we were thinking untheocratic thoughts. It was difficult to focus on the talks that we had heard many times before. Our minds wandered and searched for something to offer us a bit of entertainment.

Once Ellen was browsing through the Revelation book. She was fourteen at the time.

She stifled a giggle, cleared her throat and pointed at the book. I read it but didn't understand. She tapped impatiently at the English title. *Revelation — Its Grand Climax At Hand!*

For two or three seconds, we were perfectly impassive.

Then we exploded into hysterical laughter.

Of course, we got ice-cold stares and were told off during the intermission. But the hand climaxes were immediately included in our canonized list of double entendres.

An elderly sister once made a mistake that became a classic. Someone posed the question of what scientists thought was the origin of organisms, and she answered with a clear voice that scientists didn't understand the origin of orgasms, but in fact, all orgasms, both micro orgasms and bigger orgasms, were created by God. In a couple of weeks the story spread to the neighboring congregations, and after the circuit assemblies that summer, it was all over the country. It's still retold, even all the way in the US.

We thought we knew everything about these things. We didn't have any real experiences, of course, unless you included hand climaxes. They indeed should have been included because they could lead to homosexuality. We learned that when Brother Ekholm was disfellowshipped.

It wasn't that often somebody got disfellowshipped, at least not from our congregation, but when it happened, it usually had to do with sex. Occasionally the reason could be apostasy or tobacco smoking, but mostly it was about adultery or premarital relationships. Or post-marital relationships, as when Sister Grönblom, widowed at the age of forty-three, fornicated with a vacuum salesman who one day unexpectedly stood behind her door explaining in lovely words how clean everything would be if you used an Electrolux.

The reason why somebody got disfellowshipped was never mentioned officially. It was a short, matter-of-fact announcement that so-and-so wasn't a preacher of the word anymore. But after some time, an elder gave a talk about some urgent matter and then everybody knew the reason.

Brother Ekholm was an unmarried man in his thirties. He had several times applied to serve at the Branch Office but was never accepted. He worked in the K-Supermarket in Herttoniemi, cutting meat for our beef stroganoff and helping us selecting sausages that contained no blood. We never thought there was anything peculiar about him, but he did pay particular attention to his appearance.

One week after he got disfellowshipped, Brother Lassila gave the talk.

"Homosexuals are not born that way," he declared and pointed at an article in the magazine. "Their behavior is learned. Any homosexual can become a heterosexual. As the apostle

Paul said, that is what some of you were, but you have been washed clean. Many homosexuals claim that they were born that way. In other words, they say that the Bible is wrong."

He read the explanation for the phenomenon.

"The parents of a homosexual are often a domineering mother or a distant father. A son will never become a homosexual if his father supports his masculinity."

He frowned at us.

"Masturbation is no harmless habit. It leads to homosexuality."

We had had no idea that Brother Ekholm was gay, and we only had a vague idea of how all that worked technically. We even felt pride that we had a fag in our congregation. Brother Lassila encouraged us to tell him if we knew anybody else who had that kind of inclination. It was important that the elders got to know who they were so that they could be helped.

After this, we no longer greeted Brother Ekholm. We switched to using the T-Supermarket instead so that we would be no part of his sins. If we met him in the street, we turned our heads away.

Brother Ekholm never wanted to return to the congregation, but some other disfellowshipped persons did. In that case, they had to come to the meetings for a long time, sometimes for more than a year. They had to sit in the last row and never talk to anyone until the day came that the elders decided that they were repentant enough and could be reinstated. Everyone patted their back and said that they were so glad that they had returned. They had known all the time that God would let them see the error of their ways and repent.

I didn't know what I wanted from girls. Just to see the back of a neck under a hair bun could create a lump in my stomach.

Sex was unthinkable—that belonged to another world. It was like Upper Volta or Outer Mongolia, a distant and dangerous place that certainly existed but where nobody actually had ever been.

I lived in a loving community, with my parents and my three sisters. I knew I was safe, I knew we had the truth, I knew I belonged to the Great Crowd, God's chosen people. I knew that we were no part of this world. I was lucky to be born into a family that knew the truth.

I knew that there would always be someone to love me, but I assumed it could be difficult to find someone who wanted to sleep with me.

This was youthful optimism. It proved to be other way round.

18

A couple of years after we got married, I learned that Debra had an affair.

We had moved into a two-bedroom house in the northern part of McCook. We had a simple garden that was Debra's domain. She planted new plants, then moved them to another spot because the first spot was too sunny or too much in the shadow or didn't contain the right amount of lime. My role was to dig holes and push wheelbarrows. When I couldn't help her due to my trips, a newly arrived brother in the congregation came to her assistance.

Once I saw them by accident when I returned earlier than planned. I had been to Lexington to talk at a funeral, and since I had plenty of time afterward, I chose the northern route back for a change. I took a wrong exit, and I saw Debra's car in a driveway.

I parked a bit farther down the street and waited. Half an hour later, Debra exited the house. The brother also exited; they held hands. Debra's blonde hair was perfect. The man's chest was bare and shiny with sweat as if he just had mowed the lawn.

I thought that they looked good together, Debra with her tan and the muscular brother who resembled a football player. He opened the car door for her, and they kissed.

I felt almost nothing. I didn't even think of attacking him or creating a scene.

I followed Debra. She didn't drive directly to our place, instead, she drove by the golf course, and I thought she was on her way to meet a friend. But it turned out that she made a detour around the town and turned toward our house after she had passed the airfield. It seemed she also sometimes took the longer but more interesting route.

I killed time by driving around for an hour before I went home.

I said nothing. A confrontation would have ended either with a denial or a confession, and both would have been equally embarrassing. I tried out the word "forgiveness," but there was nothing to forgive, as I didn't feel violated. It was only a matter of physical attraction. The man probably worked with repairing tractors or grain elevators connected to the wheat silos and probably spent his evenings with his friends at Old Fort Pub. Debra would soon get tired of him. And since she had her little adventure, I could take my liberties too. I didn't do it then, though.

A couple of weeks later Debra told me one morning that she had a lot to do that day. We were having breakfast together, which was unusual.

She gave a detailed account of how she would spend the day. She would visit her half-sister, who had moved to McCook, and then she would buy a bush trimmer.

"And then I will have lunch with, eh, Cindy."

"With eh-Cindy?" I said and looked up from my morning paper. "Why are you telling me all this?"

"No reason. I just wanted you to know what was going on."

I felt like saying: Debra I know what's going on. I saw you. "Say hello to eh-Cindy," I said instead.

In principle, I was a rank-and-file elder, but I got more and more privileges, like giving talks at funerals. Perhaps they thought that my European heritage made me a bit more interesting than the dependable but uninspiring elders who only reluctantly accepted this kind of assignments. During the funerals, I talked with a relaxed voice, without any notes. That gave an impression of my talk coming from the heart. I usually interviewed the next of kin in advance, but often, one telling detail was enough to create the illusion that I had written the speech for the deceased.

I also gave the Sunday meeting public talks in other congregations, and once I got to give a talk during a circuit assembly. That was a privilege only a few ever got.

Debra didn't get involved in my dealings.

Sometimes I stayed overnight in another town, even though I could have driven home. I would get a room at a hotel and sit in a diner, watching people, inventing stories about their backgrounds.

Sometimes I brought a book and a picnic lunch and drove out on the prairie. I parked my car and had a few hours to myself. Sometimes I would get up in the middle of the night and drive around on the prairie. I rolled down the side windows, drove in high speed on the deserted, straight roads. The dashboard gleamed in the dark. I turned to byroads, to the right, to the left, randomly. I ignored the stop signs. The radio played country music.

*

When I got the opportunity to move to Carlsbad, California to become the overseer of a newly founded congregation, I thought that it might be a fresh start.

The congregation in Carlsbad had grown too big. A congregation with more than a hundred publishers was difficult to manage so it would be split up. Sometimes there would be problems with the split, particularly when the elders encountered resistance to change. It wasn't always clear who was allowed or forced to move to the newly founded congregation, and that sometimes ended in competition between brothers. In that case, it was wiser to appoint an outsider to be overseer.

At first, I was disappointed because I had hoped to be moved to Brooklyn, but Debra was enthusiastic. She always wanted to get away from McCook. She wouldn't miss anything; the muscular brother had just been a pastime.

Chris Huebinger helped us stow our belongings in the U-Haul I had rented.

"Don't forget your old friend, now that you move to the big world."

"Brooklyn is the big world. Carlsbad is far away from there."

"The way to Brooklyn is long and narrow," Chris admitted. "Carlsbad is a suitable intermediate stop."

He gave me advice.

"Make sure they don't forget you in California, or you'll never get to Brooklyn. You have to get on the fast track. And take part of the bread and the wine during Memorial; it's never a bad idea to be one of the anointed. And don't have any children."

Chris was right. Everyone who was somebody in Brooklyn was anointed. And no families with children were allowed to work in the headquarters.

The next spring, I tasted the wine and the bread for the first time. I could feel how the Carlsbadians discreetly observed me when I lifted the silver goblet to my lips. Nobody commented or asked anything. It was a personal choice; everyone knew in their heart if they belonged to the anointed. I had decided to be one of them.

I also visited a Californian clinic to undergo the procedure Chris had recommended. For a week, I felt as if I had a cactus growing under my bladder.

19

I was fifteen when I took part in the building of the Puotin-harju Kingdom Hall, the first-ever quickly built Kingdom Hall in Helsinki. We were all eager to see how the hall would e-merge from scratch into a wholly finished structure in a single weekend.

My father developed the method.

"Most of the time on a construction site, you are just wait-ing," he once explained to me. "You wait for something to dry, for material to get delivered, for the previous phase to get finished. If you plan a construction project so that every-thing is ready in time and everything is done in the right se-quence, you can erect a building in three days."

In the beginning, nobody believed him, but he created schedules, lists, work instructions, role descriptions, and charts that proved him right. The essence of the method lay in the fact that we had an infinite amount of volunteers. The first real-life trials were a bit chaotic because there were hundreds of willing but inexperienced volunteers, but as the supervisors learned the method, it proved to work. We had already finish-ed two Kingdom Halls up north in Savo and Ostrobothnia.

We began one early Friday morning in Puotinharju with prayer, the daily text, and breakfast. Whole families had ar-rived in their caravans, and there were busloads of volunteers from all over the country. The foundation had been laid earlier. The concrete base was pre-cast and had been allowed to dry. There were penetrations for the plumbing and electricity. The building materials were already on the site and had been moved to the assigned locations and labeled.

The brothers who were trained in the method took charge of their groups, and soon the framework started to emerge. Within a few hours, the first walls were completed. At the same time, one team was building the scaffolding. The crane arrived at eleven and raised the trusses.

Professional workers did everything that required specialized skills; everybody else cleaned up, carried, lifted things. All according to my father's plan. There was no lack of volunteers, and everybody had something to do. The sisters dealt with the catering, younger brothers carried construction material. The professionals were like surgeons—they only had to stretch an arm out and, hey presto, they had a drill, a tape measure, an angle iron. Somebody was driving a sky-blue VW minibus back and forth, bringing insulation materials, a piece of pipe, or a special tool and taking away anything redundant or no longer needed.

As soon as the roof was finished, they simultaneously started working on the interior and on bricking the outer walls. The plasterboards for the ceiling were fitted into place on the farther end of the building when they already were filling the joints on the other end. A bit later, they started to paint, first the ceiling, then the walls. Bricks were laid by five different teams, and as soon as the facade to the street was ready, they fastened a sign created of separate letters: Kingdom Hall.

I had visited similar construction sites earlier with my father. He had once hoped I would be a construction engineer or at least a supervisor, but he had abandoned the idea. But he did notice that I understood the essence of his method, how you could create a smooth apparatus out of an abundance of people, where everybody had their role and participated in achieving the goal.

When we were at a construction site, Father treated me like an equal. He asked for my opinion and listened. For example, we had together arrived at the decision to keep the headcount of a team to fewer than ten, because then it was easy for everybody to remember who was on the team. We created a flow chart together that showed which activity would help fulfill the goal and which was waste. To rework something was waste, to transport things unnecessarily was waste, to have a professional do trivial tasks was waste. We had a lack of masons, but anybody could clean up, so a mason should never tidy up when he was done.

Our whole family was on site in Puotinharju. The girls and Mother were busy with the catering, while Father spent most of his time in the management barrack keeping track of the schedule. Timo Auramo and Barbara Anderson were there; practically everybody volunteered.

My task was to keep the construction site tidy. I had eight young boys helping me. They gathered and carried away pieces of timber, plastic wrapping, or remains of particle boards to the assigned spots.

One of the boys got frustrated by the endless carrying.

"This is stupid. First, we gather everything over here, then we move it to another place over there, and finally, we carry it to the middle of the site before we load it on the pickup."

I started explaining that it would be even more time-consuming to carry every single load directly to the pickup, but then I realized that he had a point. I thought about it for a moment.

"You are actually right. This is stupid," I said at the exact moment my father and the brother in charge of waste disposal arrived.

I blushed, tried to explain that my intention wasn't to criticize the management. But the method just wasn't as efficient it could have been.

"You probably have a much better idea, then," the brother in charge said sourly.

I looked at Father. I couldn't express my idea in so many words as it wasn't mature yet. Father gave me his silent permission to enter the management barrack.

I sketched my idea on paper. Instead of having a separate waste disposal area at each work point and a central collection point at the border of the property, we could establish collection points for waste bags along the road. A shuttle truck could take them to the dump. The construction material should be unpacked close to the collection points because then you could stuff the packaging material directly into waste bags without having to gather and store it first. We would save time, steps and our nerves. Besides, the construction site would be tidy at all times. In the same vein, I figured out that instead of having one central storage area for tiles, we could have four smaller ones. That would allow us to avoid too much traffic between the primary storage zone and the various construction spots.

When I was ready, I presented my idea to Father and the construction supervisor, Brother Irjala. They took notes while I was talking, but didn't ask any questions. Finally, Brother Irjala scrutinized my plan for a full minute.

He put on his yellow hard hat and put his hand on Father's shoulder.

"Let's do it. Call a meeting."

He closed the door, and Father and I were alone in the barrack. Father walked over to the huge construction layout on the wall and pinned the symbols for storage and collection points to their new positions.

20

An affluent Californian town suited Debra's temperament much better than the poor and sparsely populated Nebraska.

In the beginning, she wanted to do things as if trying to transform pictures she had seen in alcohol ads or fashion editorials into memories we could share. We dressed up and had dinners in open air restaurants with ocean views, we made a road trip to the vineyards in San Luis Obispo, we picnicked and watched the sunset on Big Sur.

This was a productive, peaceful time. We got used to the quiet life. We relocated three times in five years.

I started a cleaning business together with another brother, and it provided us a decent living because we were all hard-working, Debra and I, the other brother and his wife. In the morning we cleaned the houses of rich people, and in the afternoon we had time for the congregation. We became known for being honest and efficient.

It would be too easy to say that Debra and I didn't love each other. Sometimes we argued in restaurants and hoped that the waiter wouldn't notice. We had many "we should talk" talks, often in the car, as it was easier to watch the road than to look each other in the eyes. The bedroom was the demilitarized zone—we refrained from starting or continuing the fights in bed. Instead, we avoided each other. She went early to bed, and I lingered in my office. Silence was the most popular means of communication.

Sometimes we laughed together. We took long barefoot walks along the beach between Encinitas and Oceanside.

"Do you ever feel anything?" Debra asked once when we were sitting at the water's edge letting the waves rinse our feet.

She would sometimes ask things like that. You don't feel anything, she would say, or maybe you don't even know what you are feeling. Have you always been like that? I thought these kinds of questions were inconsiderate. There are things you have to keep to yourself.

If we quit censoring ourselves and say what we thought, we would disclose our pettiness, our prejudices, our nasty habits and strange phobias, our moments of cruelty or selfishness.

I never told Debra any details of Ellen's death, or about how everything changed. I never told her about cold nights and ice and stars or about the pain that never subsides.

Sure, Debra and I were happy in a way, but that was a fragile illusion that could be maintained only if you didn't try to express it in words. You always need a certain amount of self-delusion if you want to be happy. I wondered if other married couples had discovered that truth, too.

I certainly wasn't blind to Debra's nobler sides. She was loyal: she would have none of it if her father or some of her friends criticized me. I do believe that she tried to make our marriage work. Many of our friends considered us an ideal married couple because on the outside, Debra managed to project an image of a subservient wife. A man who isn't the head of the family can't be the head of a congregation, let alone the head of a circuit. Maybe it was to Debra's credit that I was appointed overseer for the northern circuit in San Diego.

During the years I served as circuit overseer, Debra and I visited twenty congregations, each congregation twice a year, one week per congregation. I gave the same special talk to each congregation, I participated in their elders' meetings, I gave my opinion on brothers who were considered for positions as elders.

I was rather young to be a circuit overseer, just a bit over thirty, but I commanded respect. Whenever I visited a congregation, the locals participated actively in the field service, they took notes in their black notebooks, they put their best clothes on to show respect. The Kingdom Halls were filled to capacity. I was a bit amused by the transparent attitude. I remembered from my youth how as soon as the circuit overseer was gone, everything returned to normal.

We made a trip to Finland.

Sofia already had three children, but I had trouble remembering their year of birth and who was the oldest. Three boys in the photographs, water-combed, ordered by length, in precocious suits and ties, as if they came out of a newly opened package, all from the same series. We bought them gifts during the stopover at Heathrow: something soft for the youngest, a book with animals popping out of the pages for the middle one, and a toy bus for the oldest.

Sofia and Arto lived in Turku, in a lush high-rise area some distance from the center of the city. I was surprised to see

Sofia as a grown-up woman, as a mother, as a wife. My mental image of her hadn't changed over the years. It was difficult to see in her face the five-year-old or fifteen-year-old girl I remembered as my sister. I wasn't sure if we should shake hands or hug each other. I went for the hug, but it was just a gesture my hands made, there was a good deal of air between our bodies as we tapped each other on the back.

Sofia's oldest son looked at his toy bus with an unhappy face.

"You don't live in London," he said.

"There are double-deckers in New York too," I tried.

"You don't live in New York."

"We may move to New York one of these days," I said.

Sofia and Debra got along well. Sofia wasn't fluent in English, but somehow the women found each other. Debra took interest in Sofia's children, and when the youngest one showed her his toys, she clapped her hands as if he had done something truly remarkable.

Arto wanted to go out on the balcony, drink whiskey and talk man talk with me. He gave me too much unrequested information, small confidential details of his marriage and of Sofia's qualities I knew about but didn't want to discuss with a man who was practically a stranger to me.

He told me about Bellevue and how they had run electricity both to the cottage and to the sauna. He had built a terrace around the house, and a new shed. They had had a cat for the summer. They had to put it down in the fall because they couldn't have a cat in the city. Arto told me that he hit the cat in the head with a stone, but when it didn't die immediately, he took it to the jetty and kept its head under water until it drowned.

"I didn't want it to suffer. That would have been cruel. Do you understand?"

When we continued to Helsinki, I visited Carola and her husband, Rolf. Carola had almost finished her architecture studies, and Rolf was an attorney. I gave their son Max a London bus that I bought in a department store. To Rolf, I gave a bottle of tax-free cognac. I didn't tell Debra about my visit, since she wouldn't have understood, I just told her that I had to take care of some family matter.

Rolf told me his view about the break-up in our family.

"This is ridiculous. Carola hasn't met Sofia or her parents for fifteen years. If we sit down and discuss this, we surely will find an acceptable solution," he said, the professional negotiator that he was.

"You know nothing about this," Carola said.

"You should get yourself examined," Debra said when we returned from the trip.

She was always talking about children. That didn't mean that we had unlimited amounts of sex; it meant that we kept an eye on the thermometer and carefully chose the prudent time for it.

According to her examination results, there was nothing wrong with her. Now it was my turn to get tested. I would have to lock myself in a clinical room with a bunch of girlie magazines and a plastic cup. I did it, though I knew what the outcome would be.

"I'm sorry," I told Debra when I got the result. I showed her a printout with diagrams and tables and numbers circled with a red pen.

That night Debra cried herself to sleep. When I tried to approach her, she turned her back to me. There's no point, was her nonverbal message.

During my years in California, I stayed continually in contact with Ron Miller. I wrote letters and called him from time to time. He was receptive to my advances, but he said I had to be patient. Occasionally I would get writing assignments. Mostly he sent me an outline and some Bible verses, and my task was to write an easy-to-read and unambiguous text for the magazine. The text would then be edited by some unknown brother who corrected any mistakes and tailored the article into the context of the magazine. Our writing process was group work, even though we didn't know who the other persons were.

Sometimes I wrote short entries for the "Questions From Readers" column. Miller gave me the topic, and I made up a question and wrote a suitable answer. That was the way we handled communication about matters that didn't warrant a full-length article. Sometimes real questions from readers were sent to the headquarters, but they were of course never addressed in the pages of the magazine. They were sent to the congregation so that the local brothers could guide and correct the asker directly.

Sometimes I had to write two different versions of the same article. One such article was about whether or not the innocents killed in Sodom and Gomorrah would be resurrected.

"We can discuss this as long as we want," Miller said when I called him trying to figure out which interpretation was the final one. "But when it's printed, it's the truth. You write, we'll take care of the rest."

I wrote both versions, and after they had taken a vote, the Governing Body decided which version to publish. I don't even remember which it was.

It took several years before I got my ticket back to Brooklyn.

I visited an assembly in Cedar Point at the same time Ron Miller was there, and we decided to meet. We exchanged news, I told him about my life in California, he told me how he was struggling with the organizational model. The president had passed away, and his successor was George Friedman. The choice had proven to be a mistake.

"Friedman is a clown," Miller said. "He has no concept of modern leadership, and he's unable to make decisions. He wants to keep control over all the commas and every single receipt. He thinks that delegating means loss of power."

I told Miller about an article I'd read about the organizational structure of *The New York Times*. I thought there were similarities.

"The chief editor is responsible for the content and is accountable only to the readers. The CEO is responsible for the economy and for administration and is accountable to the shareholders. You shouldn't mix those two roles."

"You can't run our organization that way."

"We are in the magazine and newspaper business, too."

Miller shook his head.

"I don't like the idea of separation of duties. An organization of this size must be led from above. If you leave too much power to components of the organization, they become selfish and competitive, and that is disastrous."

I leaned forward. This was my chance. I didn't want to stay in California, but I also didn't want to just print books in Brooklyn.

"Our president has too much power. You think so your-self. We could give the president responsibility for finances, administration, and juridical matters. But the responsibility for the content of books and magazines, for spiritual leader-ship and doctrine, would belong to the Governing Body."

"The organization has three hundred voting members. You would have to convince all of them."

I knew Miller. I could see in his eyes that the root of an idea was taking hold.

Three weeks later, Miller invited me to Brooklyn for a few months to secretly plan the organizational change.

During the last ten years, the city had been cleaned up. There were no graffiti on the trains, and many of the streets now felt safe. I visited the corner of Willow Place and Joralemon Street and felt a warm rush when I saw my old window.

My second term in Brooklyn lasted four months. We laid the foundation for the new organization. We hired consul-tants to help with the change leadership and lawyers to help us minimize the tax consequences. We created a new corpo-ration, Kingdom Support Services, Inc., to take care of vehicles and smaller real estate like Kingdom Halls. The official reason for the change was cost efficiency, lower taxes, and better de-cision making. The real reason was to limit the president's authority.

A number of brothers thought that a model with two lead-ers would lead to schisms or even end in splitting up the or-ganization. They rooted for conservative central leadership.

"Be careful with Ron Miller," Chris Huebinger said when I called him in Nebraska and told him about the plans. "Miller is an old organization fox. He uses you as a tool, and your only payment is some vague promise of assignments in the future. You do the hard work and even feel indebted. If everything goes well, he'll take the credit for instigating the change. If they vote against him, you'll take the blame."

In Brooklyn, I got acquainted with a woman from Boston who was an internal auditor for a fast-food chain. Her job was to read lists, check numbers against other lists, and mark anything that didn't compute. Sometimes she had to travel to this or that office to inspect the accounts in person. Her areas were the northeastern states and parts of Canada. We always met when she visited New York, four or five times a month. She was friendly and unassuming, and we didn't get on each other's nerves.

This wasn't a great passion. We had lunch together and then we went to her hotel room to have regular American sex. Her lovemaking was like the food her employer served, of even quality, predictable, no exotic spices, medium serving temperature. Satisfying, easy to digest, forgettable, fast. The pleasure was not in the new or the acrobatic: it was in the fit of body parts, in the distribution of mass, in hydraulics, self-control, and rhythm.

We got used to each other, and I was miserable when the change management project came to an end and it was time for me to go home to California.

When Ron Miller called me a year later and invited me back to Brooklyn, I didn't have to think it over at all. My role description was a bit vague, it would be defined more precisely later on, but essentially, I was to be Miller's operative assistant.

Now that the Immigration Act was in effect, my work permit was also secured.

When I told Debra that I had permanent employment in Brooklyn, we had an argument. At first, we calmly discussed the relocation and the living arrangements, but then the discussion got sidetracked to other things. When we no longer were focused on the topic, we disclosed naked truths. We didn't listen to each other, we mined our memories for ammunition and in the heat of the fight, we said things that were too honest and too true.

"You're not even a true believer," Debra said. "You are like the worst kind of Pharisee. You belong to the organization only because you can't find anything better, you have no education and no skills, you would be nothing without the organization. You are just seeking Brooklyn's validation."

"And you think you live in the truth, but you don't even know the truth. You want me to tell the truth? How much truth do you want? Do you want me to tell what I think of your mother? What I think of you? I can tell you."

"No need for that. I know that you never loved me. You have never loved anybody."

"No? There is someone I loved once, someone you have never even heard of."

"She's the one you are dreaming of? You walked together in the rain and had deep conversations? Candlelight dinners and connection of souls? She's the one that can make you feel something? *Alison!*"

She uttered the name as if it was a fly that accidentally got in her mouth.

I deliberated for a second. I wanted to hurt her.

"I had an affair in Brooklyn," I said.

Debra said nothing. I could hear children play outside.

"She's thirty-two. She's not very beautiful. It's over, but it did happen."

"I don't believe you," Debra said. "I don't want to hear one word about it. Besides, you are a bad liar."

I felt like protesting but realized that it would have sounded awkward, so I said nothing.

Debra was wrong. In fact, I was pretty adept at avoiding inconvenient truths.

The next day, when we discussed the matter dispassionately, Debra told me that she wasn't coming with me to Brooklyn. She looked into my eyes, and I tried not to show that I was relieved.

A month later I moved to Brooklyn, got an apartment, did the paperwork needed for employment at the headquarters, received my access card and the keys. Finally, I was at the core of Brooklyn.

Debra stayed in Carlsbad. To others, we said the arrangement was temporary.

I considered contacting Alison. Sometimes I saw something Alison would have liked or found myself in places we had visited together. Sometimes I thought I saw her in the crowd. Sometimes I had an internal dialog with her. I realized that I was grateful for having once loved so much that it hurt when it ended.

I secretly checked her information in the HR register at the headquarters. She had moved up north a few months after we separated. There was no trace of her after that. To pry any further would have raised eyebrows.

Instead, I rekindled my relationship with the woman from Boston, but when her husband became paranoid, I let the relationship fizzle out.

21

Sometimes I estimate how old Ellen would be now, had she lived. How old would her little son or daughter be? What kind of life would she have? Would she be traveling around the world as a celebrated star soloist? Would the name Ellen Douglas be mentioned as a celebrity representative of our faith, like the two tennis sisters of Wimbledon fame, the now-dead bacteriophobic pop-singer, and the black top model?

Many years after Ellen's death, Carola and I discussed Ellen and her music. We talked about Ellen's famous concert in England. I told her how that evening I'd realized the enormous gap between my mediocre talent and my kid sister's gift. We talked about our favorite music and how we connected certain moods and occasions in life with whatever music we were listening to at the time.

We were sitting in Carola's living room, drinking wine. She had a modern music apparatus that could play almost anything from a streaming service. We played music for each other and compared the associations it created.

As grown-ups, our connections were different. Carola couldn't listen to "Warum?" by Miliza Korjus without thinking of the Estonia disaster. She couldn't listen to anything by Jacques Brel without being transported to the student life she lived in Paris. I tended to get lost in my thoughts when I listened to Dusty Springfield, Alison's favorite. A particular type of country music transported me back to Nebraska.

But when we discussed our childhood, and particularly the time around Ellen's death, our memories and the connections were identical.

During her last years, Ellen was the only musician in the family. Carola stopped playing piano at the same time I did, after Ellen's concert in England. Sofia tried playing the piano, but she gave up after a year. Mother had stopped playing when Carola and I were born. Because Ellen's music filled our home, we tend to connect many things that happened at that time, and in particular, everything that occurred during the last summer, with the music Ellen played.

"The Gypsy Girl's Dream," the Sibelius concerto, a sonata by Janáček, a virtuoso piece by Wieniawski. Ellen rehearsed them for the Sibelius competition. But at the time we also listened to the *Goldberg Variations* and perhaps a bit unexpectedly—we laughed when we both mentioned them at the same time—"Get on" by Hurriganes and "When Will I Be Loved" by Linda Ronstadt. Those were played on the radio and during parties the whole summer and the following fall. Sometimes we hummed them.

Of course, it wasn't only music that could trigger a memory as if we had looked into a box of old toys from childhood. Sometimes it was a scent, a sound, a particular nuance of a color. Some of these memories had faded into dreamlike, transparent images that we had distorted for them to fit our needs and our self-image. They were separate glimpses without context, and we couldn't date them with precision.

Other memories were well-defined and sharp. I'll always remember Ellen's confused, curious, and teary-eyed expression when, during the England tour, she met the Messiah.

The Messiah wasn't the Savior, but *Le Messie*.

Unfortunately, there is no recording of the final concert of the first overseas tour abroad made by the junior string orchestra, but there is a newspaper clipping as a document of Ellen's international breakthrough.

Ellen was the orchestra's concertmaster and soloist even though she was among the youngest in the orchestra; the oldest were in their late teens. Some parents traveled with them to take care of practical matters, but since Mother was ill again, László Király suggested that I go along instead of Mother. I was sixteen, but I was tall and looked older, and my English was decent.

The disaster that led to the triumph happened right before the last concert in a school in Barnsley. The bus stopped at the gravel courtyard in front of the school and in an instant, an uncontrolled bunch of young musicians swarmed out of the bus and scattered over the yard like billiard balls.

Ever since she was little, Ellen had learned to take care of her instrument. The violin was the first thing she was supposed to save in case of a fire. That was her own special rule. But Ellen never was practically inclined.

The bus was supposed to continue around the school and park on the other side. When the brakes puffed as a sign that the bus was on its way, Ellen realized that she had forgotten her jacket inside the bus. She banged on the door to catch the driver's attention, the bus stopped again, and the driver opened the door. Ellen left her violin case leaning on the bumper, got on the bus, fetched her jacket and gave the grumpy driver a quick smile when she got off again. The door closed, the brakes puffed again, and the engine revved. It was only when the bus had begun moving that Ellen realized that she had forgotten the most important rule: always one hand for the violin. She yelled.

I saw everything and Ellen's yelling caused me to run toward her, but it was of course too late.

The violin case fell to the ground, and there was nothing anybody could do. The violin ended up between the front tire and the gravel. The engine roared, but you could still hear how small stones pushed through the case, how the violin shattered into smithereens, how the strings snapped with a sharp metallic twang.

Ellen said nothing. She didn't cry. She didn't even breathe.

Her violin had been crushed like a beetle under a booth. The black case was flattened, pierced by splinters of red wood.

I rushed to her and tried to console her, it was just a violin, it's insured, don't cry, but Ellen was paralyzed. Her legs gave way, she fell on her knees, and I embraced her.

In a few hours, Ellen was supposed to play the solo of the last concert of the tour. She could have borrowed László Király's violin, but she acted like the thirteen-year-old that she was and refused.

As László Király and I were discussing the situation, a green Bentley drove into the courtyard.

An elderly gentleman got out of the car, a violin under his arm.

He told us that he had heard Ellen play last night in the neighboring town and now he had learned about the accident. He wanted to help. He wanted to lend a valuable violin, a genuine Stradivarius, only for this last concert, only to this talented young girl.

László Király declined the old man's offer, respectfully but firmly.

"We are talking about a thirteen-year-old," he said. "She's been playing a full-size violin only for a few months."

"We are talking about a unique talent."

"We are talking about an exceptionally thoughtless school-girl and about an exceptionally expensive violin," László Király said, shaking his head, but I could see that he wanted to be persuaded.

"We are talking about trust and forgiveness and about giving her a second chance," the old man said.

The auditorium was still empty when Ellen and I arrived. The chairs were in their positions, but the acoustics were cold, there were no people to dampen the reverberation. On a table, there was a violin case that looked like any other case, but when Ellen opened it, we could see that the content was unique. The violin rested on a bed of dark blue wavy velvet. It was of a darker shade than Ellen's. The decorative scroll was carved out of maple.

"This is the Messiah," the old man said, and Ellen didn't need a translation.

The Messiah was a Stradivarius built in 1716, and like all Stradivari, it had provenance. This particular instrument had been owned by Stradivarius' heirs and stored, unplayed, for years until a traveling Italian salesman bought it from an estate. He was knowledgeable about rare violins and realized its value, but he got so attached to the instrument that he never sold it. For many years, he told his Parisian customers about the violin, its unusual beauty, the rich red lacquer, the exquisite sound. Every year, the salesman said that he would bring the violin next year, every year the Parisians prepared to outbid each other to lay their hands on the violin, and every year, they were disappointed. Finally, they began to doubt the very existence of the violin and called it *Le Messie*—somebody you wait for, but who never appears.

The violin was stored, unused, in a private collection for years. Its second coming was in 1914, when it emerged in an auction in Belgrade and the British family Heller secured ownership of it.

That was the violin Ellen got to audition.

She applied resin to the bow, tuned the violin, adjusted the chinrest and squeezed the violin under her chin while she took a couple of long breaths. Her left hand found its place.

She lifted the bow and played a single note. She started mezzo piano and played a slow crescendo that culminated in fortissimo, and then she let the note glide back into pianissimo until the sound died in a faint whisper that still had a distinct pitch.

The note wasn't fully in tune, and the sound of the violin wasn't the best possible. But Ellen was beaming. She let the first long note morph into a phrase from a sonata by Paganini. She interrupted it and jumped into a fragment from some long forgotten étude, made a chromatic run, jumped into Vivaldi's A Minor Concerto. She played double stops, left-hand pizzicatos, a soft tremolo. She accelerated, braked, made quick jerks, tested the limits.

Ellen had one hour to get used to the instrument, tune it perfectly, learn its small quirks, seduce the sound out of it. I saw how Mr. Heller and László Király looked at each other.

At the end of the concert, the orchestra played an encore, the "Méditation" from the opera *Thaïs*, in a string arrangement. There was no harp, but László Király had written pizzicato for a string section that proved to be an acceptable simulation of the original.

Ellen played the solo. She had no trouble getting her violin heard above the rest of the orchestra, not even in that acoustically demanding auditorium. Most of the audience had no idea that she was playing one of the most expensive violins in the world, but I'm sure quite a few noticed the rich sound.

The music came to an end, the concert was over, the auditorium filled with applause. László Király bowed and gestured toward the orchestra to show that the young players were the stars, not him. Finally, he solemnly shook the hand of Ellen, soloist and concertmaster.

The applause swelled into a crescendo. There was a thunder of feet stamping the floor.

"*Encore,*" somebody yelled, and others joined. "*Bravo, encore.*"

The audience rose to their feet. Ellen curtsied, a bit bewildered.

László Király whispered something in her ear. She was to play one more encore.

Ellen smiled coyly, took the borrowed violin and stepped toward the front of the stage—and then she stumbled. My heart beat an extra beat. Would she destroy this violin too?

But she regained her balance. It looked so endearingly clumsy that the audience burst into laughter. Ellen blushed and waited for a while as the audience got seated and the buzz subsided.

Ellen sought eye contact with me and then with László Király, and she got an encouraging nod.

She lifted the violin under her chin. She focused. The audience was silent.

When Ellen played the first broken chords, you could sense unrest in the audience. Many of them knew string music, they were parents to children who played string instruments, or they played themselves. They immediately recognized the music. The choice must have caused wonder because the piece was way too long for an encore. And it wasn't children's music. It was a technically difficult and emotionally demanding virtuoso piece for a mature musician, something you would expect to hear played by Yehudi Menuhin in Royal Albert Hall. But here, the performer was a disheveled seventh-grader in a flowery dress in a school auditorium.

Ellen played "Chaconne" from Bach's Partita no. 2, and she played by heart, a remarkable achievement in itself.

With her chosen tempo, the length of the performance was thirteen minutes. We listened stunned, spellbound by Ellen's music. We didn't notice the passing of time.

Now that she played solo, it was easy to distinguish the strikingly beautiful tone. It had a deep, dark nuance that filled the auditorium. The overtones resonated under the spruce soundboard and bounced against the bottom plate and out through the two f-holes. It was as if the violin was an animal that wanted to get free. Ellen didn't have to search for the sound, she just released the energy that was trapped inside the instrument.

But the sound was a side issue. It was Ellen's musical interpretation that kept us spellbound for a quarter of an hour.

Ellen shut her eyes and seemed to forget the hall and the audience. She caressed the violin, controlled it, seduced it. The violin liked her. She and the violin melted into each other, her body functioned as part of the instrument when the low notes propagated through her hands and shoulder down to the floor. It seemed as if she wasn't actually playing, she simply followed the path the violin suggested.

Ellen had practiced "Chaconne" for hundreds of hours, but this was the first time she'd played it in front of an audience. She had practiced the advanced double stops and broken chords so well that she didn't have to think of them. She found the rhythm, the accents, and the pitch with infallible precision. She magically conjured the different voices by introducing minimal accents; she chiseled the melodies out with an easiness as if she was improvising.

But the "Chaconne" was no improvisation; it followed a stringent architecture that Carola once explained to Ellen and me. She said that everything was based on the power of two. There was a four-bar set of chord changes, sixty-four variations on those changes, a total of two-hundred-fifty-six bars. The first degree, second, fifth, first again, sixth, fourth, first, seventh and then everything again from the beginning. Sixty-four times.

Ellen had no interest in mathematics, she just played. She approached the "Chaconne" as if she were mixing colors, accentuating hues, creating contrasts. She introduced details I had never heard before; she created breathlessly long arcs, sharply defined figures. In Ellen's interpretation there were traces of the mathematical sharpness Carola had suggested, but essentially the interpretation was somber, almost tragic.

When the music came to an end, Ellen became aware of her surroundings, she suddenly became shy, curtsied once and fled backstage. During the applause, she remained hidden behind the curtain.

In the audience, there was a critic from *The Guardian*. He had received a tip that it might be a good idea to go and listen to the Finnish orchestra.

Two days later, the paper published an overwhelming review. It did give kudos to the solid sound of the orchestra and to László Király as the conductor, but most of the review, nearly half a page, was dedicated to Ellen and Bach's "Chaconne."

"An air of sprezzatura" was the headline. The clipping was preserved between the pages of Ellen's musical notes in the attic of Bellevue.

22

Ron Miller and I became a team. Miller included me in his projects, and I supported him, reducing his workload by managing practical tasks for which he had no time or interest.

Miller was my friend. He was extraordinarily loyal, and he spent time and effort smoothing the paths for me. Not literally, of course. I opened the doors for him because it was increasingly difficult for him to move. He introduced me to others, kept me up to date on what was going on, and warned me when he felt it was warranted.

I helped him move when he needed a more accessible apartment. He lent me money when my mother and then Debra's father died, and I had to fly on short notice both to Finland and to Nebraska.

I was working with the extensive administrative restructuring that resulted when we separated the duties of the president and the Governing Body. Miller was the chief architect of the reorganization; I was a backstage influencer.

I also wrote articles for the magazine and parts of books under Miller's desk code. Many interpretations and minor adjustments of our teachings that people considered his were written by me, albeit under his scrutinizing eyes.

Because I was considered an excellent speaker, I also was part of the group that gave talks during the summer assemblies. Mostly I traveled around the US with my teammate, but sometimes I was elected to participate in the taxing international speaking tours.

Once I visited Finland in the capacity of a speaker. We started in Dublin and continued to Birmingham, to Nancy in France, and finally via Stuttgart to Stockholm. Helsinki was our last leg.

This was the first time I had visited Helsinki for work. The city showed its best side, the summer weather was pleasantly warm. I marked off the compulsory visits in the beginning of the week and then left my partner to his own devices.

I visited Carola and Rolf. He wanted to take me on a sailing trip and that came as such a surprise that I didn't have time to find an excuse. I joined them. We sailed around the Harmaja lighthouse and passed Pihlajasaari Island. When we sailed back along the shore, Carola explained to me how inefficiently the shores of Helsinki were utilized. The south shore was filled with storage areas, parking spaces for heavy traffic, cargo ships, and empty land where there could have been residential areas, cafés, and marinas. I told her that it looked a bit like Brooklyn.

I was invited to their home and saw the house Carola had designed for her family. It looked as I expected: modern, panoramic windows, open spaces. It was situated only a mile from where we lived when we were children.

When I had a moment with Carola, we talked about old times, about Ellen, Timo Auramo, Bellevue. I told her that our father had remarried after Mother's death and now lived in Vuosaari. Carola asked about Sofia, and I told her what I knew. I also told her that Sofia never asked about her. Carola said nothing, but I could see that she had expected nothing else. She knew the rules.

"I will meet Sofia the day after tomorrow," I said. "She and Arto are staying at the same hotel as I. They suggested that I go to the opera with them, but I told them that I was too tired, jetlag and everything."

I took a taxi from the hotel, but got off at the Finlandia Hall, because I wanted to walk the rest of the way. The area around Töölö Bay was blossoming, and the bushes smelled of flowers. I took a shortcut through the Olympic Stadium, and when I approached the indoor ice rink, I saw the apostate demonstration.

I knew there would be a demonstration. They had warned me that the Finnish apostates would try to sabotage our assembly. Some of them took advantage of our lax security and sometimes managed to stir unrest inside the assembly hall before they were removed.

We knew that the apostates had built a worldwide association that had its roots in the US. They had a steering committee consisting of ten or twelve members, all former leaders in our organization. They probably felt that they didn't have enough power and in frustration, they had built their own organization that tried to spread lies and semi-truths about us. The apostate organization had members in thirty-five countries, including Sweden and Finland and they controlled everything from Internet trolling to demonstrations. They categorically denied any central governance and the very existence of the apostate organization, but we had the proof.

I decided to include a few words about how the anger and quarrelsome malice of the apostates, in fact, proved that we had the truth.

Before my talk, I retired backstage to the rooms where the A-listed speakers could relax and get ready. I examined my room. The brother in charge of the venue had done his job. I had asked for bottles of Pommac because these were not available in the US and a six-pack of Brooklyn Lager that was difficult to obtain in Finland. The furniture was designed by Alvar Aalto, the chocolate was Fazer's Wienernougat. I had asked for the chocolate only for my guests as I didn't like chocolate much. Ten fresh roses in a vase, two newly published novels on a side table. I wouldn't have time to read them here; I intended to read them on the flight home.

The VIP brother knocked on my door.

"Is everything all right, Brother Douglas?"

"One thing is missing."

The young brother was taken aback, and he consulted his list.

"But I have checked everything. What's missing, Brother Douglas?"

"I ordered a brunette, five foot seven, thirtyish, B cup."

That was a standard joke I usually told just to see the reaction. For several seconds his face was naked in shock, but then he got it. He smiled broadly, chuckled nervously, and pointed a finger at me.

The talk went as I expected. The audience was beside themselves that "our boy" had risen to a prominent position in Brooklyn and they gazed transfixed at my lips as if I were capable of telling them the exact date of Armageddon and was about to give them the password for survival.

I was the errand-boy of the headquarters, but I got the Big Chief treatment, and I can't deny it felt great.

The supply in Helsinki was average. A few well-groomed fifty-somethings still visited the gym and the hairdresser. While they were sure things, they represented no challenge. A dazzlingly beautiful twenty-five-year-old, who would prove to be impossible—she considered herself an exception who had the right to skip lines and get free drinks. I avoided that type of princess. They were like the dessert buffet at hotels, they never tasted as good as they looked.

The supply was almost invisible but perceptible to the trained eye: flowing hair, quick smiles and nearly indiscernible nipples under thin summer dresses. The women fawned on me and others from Brooklyn, as if our physical proximity could sprinkle a little power or glory.

Most of them gave me only a passing, indifferent look, the kind of look you give a celebrity when you don't want to be too intrusive or when you don't want to show that you have recognized him. Some of them came closer, touched a sleeve, or took photos of themselves with me. I was like the bearded woman at the circus whom they had the right to gawk at because they had bought a ticket.

Some women were hunting. They were alone, but sometimes I would later find out they were married. From their faces, you could conclude that their lives hadn't turned out as they had expected. Some of them had got caught in unhappy marriages and were forever bound to their good-for-nothing husbands. Some had withdrawn into their shells when they were deserted by their only true loves ten years earlier, and now they looked at younger and more attractive women with hatred in their eyes.

They wanted admiration, to taste the life in the center of power. Some of them were or had been stunningly attractive women who were now painfully aware that their assets were losing value.

I knew how to handle this kind of women. I knew how to talk to them, I knew what they needed. Some of them were best approached with a gentle, fatherly touch, while others wanted to take care of a little boy.

Seduction is not difficult. You just have to give the other party an excuse for doing whatever she wants to do.

This time I chose a woman who, from a distance, could have been anything between thirty and fifty. Only a closer look revealed the wrinkles around her eyes, permitting a better estimate. Then you could also see the sweet Finnish country girl she once was. I noticed her for the first time during my talk. She was sitting in the third or fourth row, to the left from the stage, as if she knew that the speaker's eyes often landed there. I made eye contact with her a couple of times during my talk, and the game was on. She nodded once when some part of my talk seemed particularly poignant.

I saw her again during the intermission as I was talking with a couple of brothers from a local congregation. She stood a bit away from me, alone, turned half away. A moment later, when I stood in line at the literature counter, she was close to me, browsing a book.

I enjoyed this phase of the mating game when everybody played innocent. Nobody made the first move, and both parties could maintain that nothing was said or done, that every gesture or word could have a neutral explanation. Someone had to take the inevitable step that sent an unmistakable signal. A grip of the hand, a kiss, a word. She knows. I know that she knows. She knows that I know.

Her car had once been an upper-middle-class vehicle, but you could perceive years of wear and neglect. On the outside, the car was clean but full of scratches and dents from careless parking. The leather seats were shabby, and the artificial pine forest scent inside the car was probably better than the smell it was designed to conceal. But the car had a beautiful, curved design. A classic. Debra's father would have said that they don't make cars like that anymore.

She fastened her seatbelt and waited for me to fasten mine before she drove off. She kept her hand in the ten-to-two position, leaning forward as if the car was new or the city unfamiliar. But when she turned onto the main road, she floored it. The automatic gearbox kicked down, and the engine roared like a lion.

We tumbled into my room, leaving a heap of clothes on the floor, and threw ourselves on the bed. I lit the reading light. A dim indirect light fits the illicit mood, and it's more flattering to the naked body. In low light the looks don't mean much, and the skin of an ordinary-looking woman is also warm. These women had had a strict upbringing and low self-esteem, and they were unsure of their bodies. They were inexperienced and clumsy, and afterward, they seemed frustratingly guilty and troubled.

My telephone vibrated, I glanced at the screen. Sofia.

"Go ahead and take the call," she said.

"It's not important," I said and turned the phone off.

The moment was gone, but we pretended not to notice. I kissed her again. I already had regrets, her skin was a bit sticky, and my erection was joyless. She didn't seem turned on either, her moans seemed politely contrived, but we played our parts by the book. Afterward, it felt as if we had performed a compulsory formality. We assured each other that it was all good.

"I assume you are not the kind of type that calls back," she said later when she was on her way.

"Yes," I admitted. "I don't think I am."

These women usually knew what they were doing, even though I sometimes got the impression that they were hoping for something more. They would forget their sunglasses or earrings in my room to have—or give me—an excuse to make contact again.

"But perhaps you'll return someday," she said.

Like all of us, she was looking for love, but when she couldn't find that, she settled for hope and faith.

I watched through the window as she walked over the parking lot to her beautiful but worn-out car. She opened the door but didn't get in immediately. She looked up at the hotel, her eyes searching for the right window. She stood indecisively for a moment, looking a bit lost, like the last bag on the conveyor belt at the airport.

As always, the idea of a strange woman seemed better than the actual event. Maybe I thought that if I slept with someone, I would be able to love her. The concept worked in the realm of imagination when you didn't have to consider practical matters.

*

After I had showered, I called Sofia.

She answered the call at once.

"Markus," she said. "Could you please come up to our room?"

I heard an undertone in her voice that I couldn't decipher. I wondered if she was sober.

"Don't ask. Just come. I need your help."

I couldn't remember when Sofia had ever needed my help.

Their room was on the fourth floor in the same hotel. The door was already a bit ajar, the way you leave it when you are expecting somebody.

The room was dark, the curtains were closed, and the television was turned off. At first, I thought that Sofia must have left the room for some errand, but then I could make out that she was sitting on the bed with her back to me.

"Come in, leave the light off."

In the low light, I could see that she wore an evening gown suitable for a night at the opera, but her hair wasn't done, it hung out. The room hadn't been aired out for some time, and I could smell alcohol.

I asked what had happened.

"Nothing out of the ordinary," she said.

We remained silent for a while.

"Where is Arto?" I asked.

"We had a fight, Arto and I. It was a stupid fight, as usual. We were waiting for a taxi in the reception and Arto thought that I was flirting with the concierge and I got mad. I certainly didn't flirt with him, I had barely noticed him. So I decided to show Arto what real flirting is. It was a dumb thing to do, but I went to the reception desk to talk with the man. Arto got furious and went straight to the room, he said he didn't want to go to any damn opera. You know how he can be when he has had a few glasses. After a while, I went after him, I wanted to apologize and convince him to go. The tickets were rather expensive."

Sofia lit the lamp. Her chapped upper lip made her look like she was sneering, a lopsided smile that went almost all the way up to the bruised swollen left eye. Her makeup had run down to the cheeks, sloppily wiped.

Her dress was stained with blood. Her hair was bloody. The towel on the floor was bloody.

I got up.

"Did he hit you?"

She sighed wearily as if she had given up expecting anything more long ago.

"No, of course he didn't hit me. I fell down the stairs."

Her nose was bloated.

I reached my hand out, but she withdrew.

"I'm okay. It's nothing serious, just scrapes and blood."

"You have to report him."

She sat down at the desk and reached for the mirror. She touched a clotted wound above the eyebrow.

"It wasn't the first time, either. Remember when you were supposed to visit us one midsummer? And the children got ill?"

"That was years ago."

She turned away.

"I'm gonna be okay. I always have the children."

"What a jerk. Did you ever talk about this to anyone? To the elders?"

I saw in the mirror that she rolled her eyes.

"The elders? What good would come out of that? Arto is an elder himself. Sometimes I wonder what's going on inside your head. Goblins and trolls? Fairies? Peter Pan? You don't air your dirty laundry in public, as you know. Everybody has their own problems. This happens to be mine. It's not always this stormy. Your marriage isn't exactly ideal either."

"I have never hit Debra."

"I'm sure of that. You wouldn't dare."

She looked up.

"Sorry. I didn't mean it that way. You have never been prone to violence. I just mean that you are in no position to tell me how to manage my marriage. Debra has told me a few things."

"Told you what?"

She sighed again, the unbearable sound of endless patience.

"Who do you think you are fooling? Debra has a certain confidence in me. We call each other every now and then, and sometimes she emails me. Jeanette. Maggie. That Icelandic woman. You think she doesn't know?"

Debra couldn't possibly know even half of it, but I was surprised she knew names. Information is like water, it will always seep through its own channels.

"That's none of your business."

"You are right. Absolutely right. That's my point, it's none of my business. And my life with Arto is none of yours. But I hope you could help me now. I can't go out like this, and I can't ask anybody else for help. You have to go to a pharmacy or to the reception and get a bandage and some antiseptic liquid. And you'll have to help me with the dress, I can't get it off by myself."

"I'll kill him."

"Markus, honey. Don't be melodramatic. You would never kill anybody."

23

Ellen and her best friend Barbara Anderson were baptized the summer after the concert in England. Ellen was fourteen, Barbara fifteen. They studied the yellow book and answered all the questions posed to those desiring to get baptized and one rainy afternoon during the assembly in Vaasa, they attended a functional ceremony where Brother Lind submerged them and five others for a second into the hotel swimming pool. Before that, they had promised eternal obedience to God's earthly organization. Carola and I had been baptized a couple of years earlier and Timo several years before that, so now all of us were full members of the organization. We would never be able to leave without facing severe consequences.

As far as I know, Ellen never lost her childhood faith. Until her death, she was convinced that God very soon would wipe out the wicked world and that we would live in a paradise before she was a grown-up. Her greatest fear was that she would accidentally commit a sin that would prevent her from surviving Armageddon.

During the assembly in Vaasa, Ellen also played a part in a Bible drama.

The dramas were the highlight of the assemblies. Mostly they were full-costume dramas that retold a biblical story.

We were supposed to draw some parallel with the present from these old dramas, but sometimes the connection remained unclear. But we liked the shows. When the program was boring, the dramas enlivened our day.

Originally Mother was supposed to play a part in the drama, but as usual, her health didn't permit it. Her fatigue was deeper than usual. I just can't manage it, she said and left the chores to us. She locked herself in the bedroom with the curtains drawn, and Father had to sleep on a mattress in the kitchen. She would see shadows and hear steps, and she slept during the days and was awake during the nights. We couldn't flush the toilet, because Mother would wake up. We couldn't vacuum clean, Mother would wake up. We couldn't talk loudly, Mother would wake up. We could, however, play music. Ellen's violin didn't bother her in the least.

The brothers reckoned that Mother needed a stronger faith and more Bible guidance, so they made a shepherding call. Mother opened the door in her nightgown. The apartment was untidy, and the air was stale because Mother didn't want to keep the windows open due to the traffic noise and the soot. When she saw the two brothers in their suits, perhaps she could see herself through their eyes, a tired and tetchy half-dressed woman with unwashed hair. She reacted by throwing the phone catalog at them and yelling that they had no business visiting uninvited. They backed off into the staircase, and she closed the door with a bang.

We didn't get any help because there was no medicine, there was nothing physically wrong with her. She just had to pull herself together and study the magazines more intently.

They never talked about Mother in the congregation. Sharp edges should be softened, flaws should be erased or at least ignored so that we would fit into the picture of how a family was supposed to look like. The Douglas family was a happy family, no doubt about that, and all signs of weakness were giving bad witness and a proof of lack of spirituality.

This assembly drama was about David's daughter Tamar and her brother Absalom and half-brother Amnon. Ellen played Tamar. Barbara was Tamar's maid who helped her cook heart-shaped cakes and bring them to the interior room of her half-brother. Because Mother was ill, Barbara's mother played her role as the king's concubine. The tale was a typical Bible story, cruel and violent. The half-brother raped Tamar, and her brother killed the rapist.

The brother who led the rehearsals suggested initially that Barbara should play Tamar and Ellen the maid. That would have been suitable as Barbara was older than Ellen. But Ellen wanted to play Tamar and Barbara also preferred the role of the maid.

"I know that the part covers adult topics that require life experience," Ellen said to the director. "But I'm emotionally mature, and bodily integrity is important to me. I'm sure I can make a credible Tamar."

I sat with Carola and Sofia in the first row. The actors wore clothes that matched the depicted time, and they lip-synched to a playback tape. Ellen had fixed her hair before the performance and decorated her dress with a piece of red glass, representing a ruby.

The rape was of course never shown, you just had to figure it out based on Tamar's actions and because her clothes and her hair were messy and the ruby was gone. When her brother later killed the rapist, that was also only hinted at. The stage bathed in muted ice-blue light representing night.

After the performance, we congratulated Ellen and Barbara. During the rehearsals, neither of them had shown any talent. They hadn't known what to do with their hands and gesticulated wildly instead. They acted acting. During the actual performance, something happened. Maybe it was her gorgeous dress, her lead-part-prompted self-confidence, the spotlights and the support from the thousands in the audience that made Ellen bloom. She performed the part the same way she played the violin, she controlled the stage, she delivered her lines like a small but world-famous diva. When I looked at her, I suddenly realized that my sister had become a young woman.

24

In addition to contemplating about how Ellen's life would have been, I also think about my own life, the choices I have done or avoided doing. If I had stayed with Alison, or if I had never come to Brooklyn. Or if I hadn't married Debra, or if we had had children.

It's fruitless to speculate. It would be wise not to think about things that could have been, to compare the current to something fictive, something possible, something that is already lost. But I still do it.

I visited California a couple of times per year, and I liked the climate, but the lifestyle Debra had dreamed about and now could afford wasn't for me.

The inheritance Debra got from her father helped her buy a small house in Huntington Beach. I stayed there when I visited California, but it wasn't my home. We were civil to and considerate of each other. We had been married for years, but our conversations sounded as if we were on our first date.

Sometimes we discussed the possibility of Debra moving to New York, or me moving to California, but we both knew that we were so used to our routines that this long-distance marriage suited us better. In practice, our marriage had been dead for years.

Ron Miller knew about the state of our marriage, but he never commented on it. He himself was unmarried, and I had never seen him even talk to a woman. He was hardly interested in men either, though he wouldn't have advertised it if that were the case. Miller had only one passion: to renew our religion.

"Our teachings are rotten. Everything we teach belongs in the dump. We have gone in the wrong direction for years. We have locked ourselves into our positions, and now we are hostages of our own doctrines. We should start with Genesis and rewrite all our interpretations."

He showed me a twenty-point reformation program that he wanted to push. It was a long list, and he had expanded every item into three or four paragraphs.

I browsed the list but expressed no opinion. I considered it dangerous to discuss alternate teachings too openly. Miller wasn't afraid of that, he knew his worth. He was seventy and had been a member of the Governing Body for a couple of years. He had already profiled himself as a tactician who wanted to tear down sacred walls. He knew that nobody loved him, but apparently, he enjoyed the fact that some of us were afraid of him.

He was now using a wheelchair, and the whole of the ninth floor had been remodeled accordingly. It was only a matter of time before he would start remodeling our teachings and make them more accessible too.

I had been sitting in my office the whole morning, sweating. The air-conditioning had broken down, and it wasn't for the first time either. Our headquarters was like a metaphor for the organization. On the surface, everything looked in mint condition, because we had covered the cracks with new plaster. Inside, everything was hopelessly dated. The electricity, the network cabling, and the ventilation were at the end of their life cycles. We had been talking about renovating the whole building, including the interior, but the costs were prohibitive, and it was difficult to find temporary office space.

I turned my computer off and went for a walk to get a some fresh air.

It was the spring after the 9/11 terrorist attacks. I walked under the Brooklyn Bridge toward the Manhattan Bridge, to an area called Dumbo. It used to be an industrial area filled with storage buildings and light industry, but recently, a hipster and artsy area had emerged, with cafés, rehearsals studios for rock bands and expensive loft apartments.

When I neared the old ferry harbor, I heard somebody play the violin. At first, I thought that it was a street musician, but then I realized that the sound came from a building close by. I recognized the music. It was the *Carmen Fantasy* by Sarasate, the one that Ellen had played at the spring matinée.

The music came from a building that looked like an old storage house. The large window on the second floor was open, but I couldn't see anybody because the musician was standing in the shadows, a few feet inside.

I stopped to listen.

The invisible violinist wasn't very proficient, or maybe she had only recently started practicing the piece. She repeatedly stopped the music, corrected her playing, made sudden pauses—probably she jotted something in her notes—and started again.

Sometimes, when you later try to reconstruct how a particular idea has formed, it seems to be just a random connection of thoughts. One's mind makes wild leaps, finds unpredictable associations, and then a new idea is born. Later it may seem self-evident.

As I listened to the unknown violinist and looked at the storage building and at the water that glimmered between the houses, I remembered how Ellen had been interested in homes with sea views in Marjaniemi and what Carola had explained about the harbor areas of Jätkäsaari and Hernesaari when we sailed along the shore of Helsinki. Since it wasn't necessary anymore for the factories to be close to water routes, or in the central part of the cities, many old industrial areas in cities had received a new lease on life. First, the abandoned buildings were taken over by hipsters and artists because they were inexpensive, and then the middle class followed. The area came into vogue, and the prices skyrocketed. That's what had happened in Greenwich Village and in the Meatpacking District. Now the same thing was happening in Dumbo and the whole northwest corner of Brooklyn.

I left the unknown violinist practicing in her storage building and hurried back to my office.

"Imagine," I said to Ron Miller a couple of weeks later during our private planning meeting. "Imagine that we sell everything off. The whole of Brooklyn."

Miller said nothing.

"How much do we own in Brooklyn? Thirty-five buildings? Four million square feet? And that's only between Brooklyn

Bridge and Atlantic Avenue. Is it the mission of the organization to own buildings in New York?"

Ron Miller had the habit of listening attentively when I presented new ideas. He asked complementary questions and nodded, but I could never be sure whether he agreed or not. Usually, he made his decisions swiftly.

Now I could see that there was something in my presentation that piqued his interest. As always, he played the devil's advocate.

"All our buildings are fully in use. We actually need more space."

I explained that our growth was faltering. In the west, it was only one percent per year, which almost exclusively consisted of children born inside the religion. If we wanted to have more growth that way, we would have to ban contraception. But our New York headquarters had grown like a cancer that sent tumors all the way to Prospect Park. We were now forced to streamline, outsource, cut costs. The Scientologists, for example, had a minimal cost level compared to ours, and they had a much higher income per capita. Our organization was inefficient, and the buildings were outdated.

"We are just rearranging the deck chairs on the Titanic," I said. "It's time to have a look at the big picture."

Miller was drawing circles on his paper, but I could tell that he was listening.

"If we get rid of Brooklyn, we could buy land in upstate New York. We could build a campus with modern buildings that are custom-made for us. Airy living, clean, close to nature. No parking problems, no difficult neighbors, no noise."

"Have you been talking to Patrick O'Hare about this?"

"No. I wanted to gather the facts first."

"Patrick is in charge of everything that concerns real estate and properties."

"Just between us: he is a conservative thinker and will kill my idea before we have had time to evaluate it."

Miller was silent for some time.

"What do you suggest?" he finally asked.

"With your permission, I'll hire a real estate consultant to evaluate every building we own and create a preliminary plan to build a campus. It's best to have everything in black and white. 'In God we trust, all others must bring data.'"

"I don't want to get into trouble with the property department."

This was the heart of the matter.

Miller did have the authority to make decisions about the planning, but Patrick O'Hare might take offense. O'Hare was a somewhat difficult person, and he didn't always agree with Miller's decisions.

"Let's let the matter rest for some time. When you come back from your tour, we'll take a closer look."

When I returned from the summer tour, Miller gave me the green light. Patrick O'Hare was furious, though he didn't show it. He still had the responsibility for other real estate matters, but I got the authority and a budget for my investigatory project.

This was my chance to show my capabilities. It was purely a preliminary survey and not a real project, but I knew that Miller was testing me. I had to succeed or else I would be an assistant forever, never making any decisions.

I started searching for a suitable property for sale. It had to be within a few hundred miles from New York, it had to have adequate connections, it had to be large enough at a reasonable price, and above all, it had to be possible to adapt the zoning plan to our needs.

I worked twelve hours a day. I attended meetings, sent emails, filled in Excel sheets, read important papers in the backseat of black cars. I had things to do, people to meet, and all the time I was in a bit of a hurry. I met realtors and immersed myself in land registries and zoning plans with the help of experts. We investigated, we got quotations, we dismissed them all.

I got a room on the eighth floor and chose a painting. I picked a Norman Rockwell that I didn't like, but which I assumed would be a safe American choice. Our storage rooms were filled with valuable paintings that we had acquired through wills, and there was a Chagall that I liked, but to choose that one would have been proof of European snobbery.

In February, on President's Day, there was a snowstorm as we returned from upstate New York after having met yet another real estate agent. It had been snowing in the morning, but when we drove back to New York City, the driving conditions became unbearable. In Finland or Nebraska, such a storm would have meant a bit of an inconvenience, but here it meant chaos. The car wasn't equipped with winter tires, so I asked the driver to stop at the nearest hotel.

I booked a room and had a cup of coffee in the restaurant. I browsed through my papers, trying to assess if the land I've seen was the right one for us.

The snowstorm was now a blizzard. I got up and stood by the window. It was a beautiful sight, though you couldn't see much, except for the snow. The courtyard was partially illuminated, and the light from the spotlight created a narrow silvery cone. The snowbanks grew by the minute. Soon the main roads would be impassable.

A woman stood next to me. She smiled at me. We exchanged a few words about the weather and watched the wild spectacle together.

I had the idea that I might take a shower, change my clothes and ask her to have dinner with me. I was unable to resist these opportunities.

She had a demure smile, and I sensed that she would be understanding, she would accept my shortcomings and re-veal her own, perhaps something trivial like that she would squeeze the toothpaste tube at the middle instead of from the bottom or that she was addicted to romantic comedies. We would make a weekend trip to the mountains. We would settle down in a small coastal town. We would start a shop together, or a restaurant or an accounting firm, because she was multi-talented and hardworking and didn't dream of a superficially high standard of living.

I turned around to say something. She was gone.

I looked around the restaurant, and then I saw her. She was sitting with a child and a man at another table, and they smiled at each other. She noticed me and waved.

I watched them in secret for a while. They seemed like a normal family, not that I knew what such a family looked like. I felt something that I had no words for: nostalgia for a life I'd never lived.

I stayed for a while at the table, but I was no longer reading my papers. I had already decided to reject this quote. The property was a bit too far away from New York City, a bit too pricey and a bit too small. Formally, the committee made the decision, but I could present it in a good or bad light. The decision was mine.

When making important decisions, one is always alone.

25

After the concert in England, Ellen's reputation spread in the music circles, and a year later she played Bruch's Concerto in G Minor with the Helsinki Philharmonic Orchestra in the new Finlandia Hall. Her name was on everyone's lips, they talked about a new Liana Iszakadze. Ellen's teacher planned for her to participate in the Sibelius Violin Competition, which would be arranged in the fall. She would be fifteen by then, which was the lower age limit.

Father objected to Ellen's participation, saying it was un-theocratic and that she was making herself important and promoting competition. But for once, Mother dared to rebel against him, and she defended Ellen furiously. Mother had been a skilled musician herself, but she had given up every-thing for the family, and now Father shouldn't stand in the way of Ellen, too. Mother went to the piano, took her framed diploma, shattered the glass and tore the diploma into small pieces. Father gave in and never said another word about Ellen's plans.

I don't think Ellen was interested in winning or achieving stardom per se, but she wanted to show her capabilities, like a climber who conquers a mountain because he can. The degree of difficulty defines the achievement.

But she was firm on one point: unless she got a better violin, she wouldn't participate in anything at all. In England, she had acquired a taste for precious violins, and even a decent violin wouldn't cut it anymore. László Király also claimed that it was impossible to reach the top with a mediocre violin.

We couldn't, of course, afford to buy a rare violin but the Savings Bank Art Foundation came to our aid. They had acquired a number of valuable instruments, including six violins, two altos, and four cellos. They lent these instruments to qualified young candidates for five years at a time. The screening was rigorous; the candidates should have merit to show and a bright future ahead of them.

Ellen got her violin during late winter. It was a genuine Guarneri, and it was the most valuable item we've ever had in our possession.

The instrument was a beautiful. You could see traces of wear, small scratches on the cover and on the fingerboard and the lacquer had faded in places, but considering its age, the instrument was in excellent condition. The Art Foundation also had a Stradivarius and a Gagliano, but this Guarneri del Gesù from 1741 was considered to be the finest in the collection.

Ellen loved her violin. She practiced for hours each day, solo sonatas and chamber music pieces for the competition's first rounds, and Sibelius' and Bartók's concertos that she would play in the finals if she ever got so far.

I always connect the events of that spring and summer with the Sibelius concerto. In the first movement, about a minute into the piece, there is a sequence that begins on the open G string and then jumps an octave up. I always got the creeps listening to the sound: a coarse, erotic snarling, deep and a little puzzling. There is no other sound like the open G string on a violin. It tickles the back of your head and raises goose-bumps on your skin. Ellen explained that Sibelius chose the key of the concerto so that he could write that particular note as a low G on the open string. If the key had been C minor instead of D minor, the note would have been impossible to play, because the violin doesn't go that low. And if the key had been E minor, the note would have landed on A, and the timbre would have been tighter and less resonant.

Ellen practiced a couple of hours after school and again after dinner unless we had a meeting that night. I often sat in my room and listened, especially when she played Sibelius.

One day in April, she was so focused when she played the concerto that she didn't notice me coming home. I went into my room to listen. When she took a break, she went to the bathroom but left the door open. After a while, I heard noises. They were so weird that I had to go and take a look.

The door was ajar, and I saw Ellen standing by the mirror. She had put her hands around herself, as if she was hugging herself, and leaned over the sink. Her eyes were closed.

The strange sound was her kissing her own reflection.

That made an unbearably beautiful and lonely picture.

This was a private moment, so I went back to my room. Of course, I never told her what I'd seen. Ellen usually hated anyone touching her, and I had naively imagined that Ellen wasn't interested in such things, that her only passion was music.

At this time, both Carola and I had our first crushes. For my part, it was completely innocent, and according to what

Carola told me, she didn't go very far either. Carola was fond of Simon Goldberg, whom she had met at her job at the Stockmann department store. Carola was a salesperson at the perfume department and demonstrated eau de colognes and eau de toilettes with a fancy French pronunciation. Simon sold radios. They dated throughout the summer, in secret, of course, because Simon was worldly.

I was interested in Paula, who belonged to the Helsinki Southern Congregation. Her congregation used the same Kingdom Hall that we used. We had the weekly meetings on different days and the Sunday meetings at different times.

During this period, young people from various congregations nearby used to come together, supposedly to study the magazine, but in fact to meet each other. Usually, an older brother would be responsible for the event. Timo Auramo often assumed the responsibility. Despite the fact that he was only twenty-one, he was already a ministerial servant and would soon start working at the Branch Office.

I participated eagerly in these events because I wanted to meet Paula. Carola was less keen because her mind was elsewhere. Ellen and Barbara Anderson also took part a couple of times, though Ellen, in principle, was too young as she turned fifteen in the spring.

Barbara was sixteen that summer. She had grown into an attractive but shy girl. She always looked scared when somebody said something to her, and she had a habit of squinting and pouting her lower lip when she was pondering her reply, and that made her look as if she was about to burst into tears.

Barbara's breasts were strikingly large, a fact she seemed to be unaware of. Sometimes she dressed in loose clothes and sometimes in short skirts and tight-fitting blouses that caused the brothers' eyes to wander and made the sisters mutter disrespectful comments between clenched teeth. It was rumored that Barbara at least once had been sent home crying from the meeting to change into something more theocratic.

In May, Barbara was disfellowshipped.

We knew even before the announcement what had happened. Ellen and Barbara had seen a movie at Bio Rex on Saturday night, and they took the same bus home. Barbara got off at an earlier stop and took a shortcut along the jogging track through the forest. There an unknown man had threatened her with a knife and "molested" her. That was the euphemism we used. The man was caught the same evening and would probably be convicted based on Barbara's testimony and the evidence gathered during the medical examination.

During Wednesday's service meeting, Brother Lassila gave a talk with the title "A Woman's Obligation to Resist."

He began by telling us about how Jacob's daughter Dina was violated when she got into bad company.

"If a woman dresses provocatively, it's evident that she has no moral compass. Mothers must share the blame. It is the mother who has the responsibility to teach her son respect for women. But many mothers have failed."

Brother Lassila told us, however, not to blame anyone.

"The victim of rape should treat the perpetrator with respect. He is a human being. She must understand that there may be circumstances in his life that have caused him to choose the wrong path."

Brother Lassila spoke like he always did, with a neutral monotone voice, without great passion. He could have been reading the financial results of the previous month. But when he quoted the magazine, the tone rose a minor third higher, as if to signal that we now were listening to the ultimate truth.

"Should a woman silently acquiesce? The rapist is asking her to consent to fornication or adultery. If she voluntarily submitted to rape, she would ruin her relationship with the congregation, and she would be disfellowshipped."

Ellen was devastated by Barbara's disfellowshipping. Now that Barbara had abandoned the truth, Ellen could no longer sit next to her at lunch or even acknowledge her.

Outside of school, Ellen secretly kept in touch with Barbara.

I met them once by accident when I was on my way home from work. They came toward me, strolling along the Etelä-satama Harbor toward Tähtitorninmäki hill. When they saw me, Barbara looked even more scared than usual. Ellen defiantly held her head high.

We stopped all three of us. Barbara didn't look at me. She said something to Ellen and then she was gone.

Ellen stayed. She looked at me with a serious expression.

"Do you know what Brother Jonsson told me?" she asked. "If you greet a whore, you'll soon be a whore yourself. Do you think I'm a whore now?"

Her face was vulnerable, but at the same time, there was an undercurrent of strength. Ellen was small in stature, but sometimes I felt that she was the strongest person in our family. That is how I like to remember her: sensitive yet strong, determined, a bit feisty.

We looked each other in the eyes. Her question was so absurd and unexpected that we both exploded in laughter.

"Say hello to Barbara," I said. "But be careful when you are out on the town. You never know who may see you."

Ellen later told me that they met in secret throughout the summer. They visited the castle of Suomenlinna, went to the movies, and made a trip to the bird observation tower in Viikki. Ellen even visited Barbara when her mother was not at home. Once Barbara visited us, on a day when Mother was fine and out on errands with Sofia. They locked themselves in Ellen's room. I made them tea and sandwiches, and Barbara thanked me politely, but she didn't look me in the eyes.

26

During the years I lived in America, I often had a feeling of being a spectator of my own life. I didn't participate, I just watched from a distance, as from a hundred feet above. All intense colors became faded pastels. I no longer felt any anticipation when I visited a new city. I wasn't excited by the thought of doing something for the first time. I had become content and a bit lazy. Things that previously had given me joy had become meaningless. Reading. Early mornings. Women. I needed something stronger to feel anything. Sometimes I thought I understood how someone could become a drug addict or a serial killer.

The only thing that gave me pleasure was when I immersed myself in a problem or task so deeply that I forgot about time and space. It happened less and less often. Not even the fact that we finally had found a suitable area of land for sale gave me the satisfaction that I had imagined.

A month after we found the land in Warwick, approximately one hundred miles north of Brooklyn, I visited Paris. After her divorce, Carola had moved there again, and she now lived in a one-bedroom apartment in the southwestern part of the city. She had decorated her home in the Scandinavian style. It was sparsely furnished in blond wood and clinical white, tasteful art on the walls, no unnecessary objects, horizontal surfaces empty. The kind of minimalism you can afford if you have an abundance to begin with.

I spread the aerial photos and drawings of Warwick over her table.

"We will demolish the existing buildings," I said. "We are building everything from scratch, but most of the area will remain in its natural condition."

Carola glanced through the sketches with an expert's eye.

"Have you thought about carbon footprints, heating, energy consumption? You could be self-sufficient regarding energy."

She asked about areas and volumes, number of users, service roads, heavy traffic, green spaces, visitors. She knew what she was doing, asked the right questions, and quickly realized the potential of the area.

"I would place the parking spaces underground. The architecture could be dramatic. The dominant element of the administration building could be a tower, like a swan neck for example, and the meeting room could be camouflaged as the swan's wings, or angel wings if that suits you better."

She outlined her idea with a few strokes. In minutes, she created a compelling study, which reminded me of the Sydney Opera House.

"Or a pine cone in glass, aluminum, and wood, something down-to-earth but elegant."

She added a few dashes so that the swan became a cone.

I understood her intention, but I didn't think it would be doable.

"The wow-architecture style is not really us. I would rather take a pragmatic perspective."

In the evening we dined out. We talked about her wrecked marriage, and I refrained from saying that divorce was the right solution. We didn't talk about my marriage. Carola had founded an architectural firm together with her friend from the early years in Paris, Valérie. She told me that their team had completed the center plan for a small coastal town. The plan was considered innovative.

Then Carola asked how our father was doing. Her tone revealed no undercurrents. But the question came as a surprise, as if a doctor, while writing down personal information suddenly asked an intimate question, lightly, in passing, not giving the issue great weight.

I remembered how Carola always helped Father in the fall when he took the outboard engine apart, piece by piece. He would spread out a sheet on the flat rock and placed each piece on the sheet in a systematic pattern. He cleaned the screws and the nuts and the cotter pins with a piece of cotton waste. He oiled what was supposed to be oiled and fit everything back together again. He was focused, and his tongue hung out and moved in sync with his fingers. Carola had a sharp memory, and when he hesitated and held up a metal part and seemed to be searching with his eyes, she would point and smile when he found the right place to fit the piece of metal in.

I said our father was fine.

That year I had a speaking tour in South America. My partner for this trip was Michael Derrick, and he brought bad news.

Michael Derrick had been appointed Administration Director for North America and had responsibility for investments. Although I did not report to him, he ultimately had the formal power to decide on the Warwick campus. We were sitting on the plane to Buenos Aires when he brought the matter up.

"Patrick O'Hare wants to lead the construction project in Warwick. You had the authority to manage the land acquisition, but now that the sale is signed, the project can be transferred to the real estate division. I have decided to do so."

This was a major blow.

I had always assumed that the project would be mine until it was finished. I had already invested hundreds of hours in the preliminary investigation and in interviewing experts. I had a clear vision of the end result, I had created a tight but realistic schedule, I had ensured that the required funds for the project were made available and, above all, I felt that I had Ron Miller's support in controlling the project.

Miller had said nothing about transferring the responsibility. On the other hand, I knew that Miller did not want to offend the real estate department.

I appealed to Derrick's vanity.

"I know that Patrick O'Hare wants the project. But do you think it is a good idea? As far as I know, it's your decision. Not Miller's or Patrick O'Hare's."

"The decision is mine, and I have now made it. I'm not going to run over Patrick O'Hare. He considers this as a coup. I'm a bit hard-pressed, I'm sure you are competent, but that's how life is sometimes. It's a pity you don't get along with Patrick. Together, you could do wonders."

"I do get along with him. He's the one who doesn't like me."

Derrick was the keynote speaker, and it was my job to support him and make sure that the arrangements went smoothly. I booked the hotels and the flights and in fact, I also wrote Derrick's speeches. I did the interviews, I searched for a proper approach and defined the Brooklyn position. Then I printed out the first version of the speech on the hotel printer. Derrick read it through, making corrections with a pen. I rewrote it, editing on the fly for language and structure. He reread it and made corrections. We kept on until the speech was ready.

But this was not my only task.

Many years earlier, Derrick has been accused of some distasteful things in a congregation in Atlanta. There were underage boys involved, and it was word against word, there were never two witnesses.

Around that time, similar scandals were exposed within the Catholic Church, and old stories were dragged to the surface. A number of lawsuits came down on us. The headquarters became wary, Derrick was deemed a risk, he was pulled back to Brooklyn, and for the following twelve years, he worked in administrative positions in the research department until the new president pardoned him and he could continue as if nothing had happened. But as his teammate, I was informed of his background and was asked to keep an eye on him lest he did anything to cast a bad light on the organization.

In practice, I was Derrick's chaperone. He accepted it without objection.

In Buenos Aires, I met Bob Sheridan, my former roommate from Brooklyn. He had become grizzled and was overweight, but otherwise, he was his usual self. He was now Argentina's coordinator, but he was also one of the candidates to become the overseer of the entire zone. Bob showed me the town, a floating Kingdom Hall in the delta area, and the Branch Office.

The Argentinian Branch Office was small, only a few hundred people. During the military junta period, our operations in Argentina were prohibited, but now the growth was steady, and Bob implied that it was at least partially due to his hard work.

We talked about our time in Brooklyn and promised to keep in touch in the future, the way you usually do when you haven't seen each other for years.

The last leg of the trip was from Peru to Brazil, to the assembly in Rio de Janeiro. We checked in at the JW Marriott, which was a five-star hotel, but because it was out of season—the hotel called it blue weeks—the price was reduced, and it was lower than for a standard three-star hotel. As such, we didn't break the travel policy that required moderation. We got two adjacent rooms with a view of the Copacabana beach.

At the Mariott, my attention lagged for a moment. We had visited a congregation and then talked to some young brothers being considered for positions as ministerial servants. When we got back to the hotel, I worked for a while in my room before dinner. Then I went down to the hotel bar to wait for Derrick.

I was sitting with a book and a glass of mineral water when I heard some trouble in the lobby: two upset men tried to explain something in Portuguese to the receptionist, who seemed to be trying to call someone. I returned to my book, but my mind wandered off to our trip home. Tonight, I would once again discuss the Warwick issue with Derrick, even though he didn't seem to want to talk about it. He wanted to give the project, my child, to someone else, without explanation and that made me furious. I had done the hard work, and now someone else would take the credit.

I sulked. I recognized in myself some of Ellen's childish traits, and I smiled a little to myself.

A moment later, the receptionist came straight to me and asked me to accompany him to the reception area.

The two Portuguese-speaking men were still standing at the counter, and when they saw me, they began to talk heatedly. I didn't recognize them but based on their clothes, I guessed they were our people. I realized that the commotion was about Derrick and that they wanted me to go with them.

We went to their car.

It was already dark, and it had started raining. This was not the Rio you could see in the travel brochures. This was wet and hot and dirty, and unsafe. We drove in silence a few miles up the mountain and stopped in front of a house. The door was wide open. They ushered me in.

In one of the bedrooms lay Derrick.

He lay naked on the floor, in a puddle of blood and vomit. I wasn't sure if he was conscious.

I felt a knot in my stomach. It was as if I had been responsible for a beach picnic, and now one of the children lay face down under the water.

A third man, apparently an elder or ministerial servant, explained the situation in broken English. It was somebody's son, someone had caught them. Derrick's nose and chin were crushed, and possibly he had cracked a couple of ribs.

My mind raced. I thought of the reports to the headquarters, the questions, the accountability, the scandal. Derrick would never recover. Neither would I.

"I'll take care of him," I said. "It is important that we do this right."

The brother looked at me the way you look at a shirt to assess if it's worth one more wash. He turned away and waved his hand.

"Go. Just go. Make sure he never shows his face in this country again."

Derrick tried to speak, but his lips and tongue were so swollen that I couldn't make out what he said.

The following morning Derrick was still in the hospital. I told the assembly managers that we had been mugged outside a restaurant and that I would give Derrick's talk.

I postponed our trip home and worked at the hotel. I canceled tickets and meetings, sorted out questions about insurance, medical certificates, and responsibilities. I also had to appease the Brazilian brothers. I visited Derrick a couple of times every day. He was constantly getting bouquets of flowers from the congregations in Rio, and he got a flower shipment from Brooklyn too.

When Derrick finally was discharged, he was full of shame and bruises. I didn't ask what had happened, but I told him that I had given his talk, handled the visits to various congregations, the reports to Brooklyn, and everything else.

He said it was customary to keep certain things within the family, not to poop in your own nest. He said that the brothers take care of each other. He said he would never forget those who were loyal to him. The most important thing, he said, was never to bring any shame to the organization.

Sometimes life is a mess and clumsy and a bit dirty. When illusions are shattered and the shady nooks of life are exposed in a revealing light, one cannot always rely on people's goodwill. But it is easy to exploit someone's heavy conscience. If you are thinking with the wrong body parts, you reap what you sow.

First, I asked Derrick to get tickets in business class, because I hate long flights in economy class. He protested. According to the travel policy, only the Government Body was allowed to fly business class.

On the return trip, we sat among businessmen in the wide seats in the front section of the plane, enjoying a premium meal. I hardly spoke to Derrick during the flight. I worked for some time on my laptop, and we slept the rest of the journey. We woke up for breakfast when we had an hour left to New York.

Once the plane had landed and was taxiing toward the gate, I said that it would be an unfortunate decision to transfer the Warwick project to Patrick O'Hare.

27

Ellen's last summer was a summer of little secrets of no importance. Carola and I had our first loves, Ellen kissed a mirror.

In July, we experienced a prolonged heat wave. A political summit held in Helsinki dominated the news. They cleaned up the city. Homeless alcoholics who slept under the bridges were moved out of sight. Long convoys with a police escort frequently disrupted the traffic and people gathered along the streets to get a glimpse of the President of the United States, the Chancellor of West Germany or the General Secretary of the Soviet Union. The international news showed a beautiful and safe Helsinki summer.

Nothing happened regarding Paula during that summer. We glanced at each other, but neither dared to make the first move. I felt immature. At night, I hugged my pillow and kissed the back side of my hand. I was waiting for life to begin, I wanted to grow up, but I didn't know how. It felt as if both Carola and Ellen were older than I, they lived in their own secret worlds that I knew about but didn't have access to.

In August, we received the news that Ellen had been accepted for the first round of the Sibelius Violin Competition.

It's difficult for me to describe Ellen's last fall and death, and how Carola left us and we abandoned her. My memories are vague. I'm no longer sure what I remember and what my mind has constructed after the fact to make my memories seem coherent.

The foremost impression is that Carola and I failed. Our responsibility was to protect each other, but we couldn't protect Ellen.

This I do remember.

Ellen began to practice a virtuoso piece that was specially commissioned for the competition. It was a modern piece, full of bizarre intervals, and I wasn't particularly fond of it. Ellen was excited about the competition piece and tried to explain it to me, but in this case, we didn't speak the same language. On some level, I understood the reasons for her enthusiasm, but I couldn't share it. To my ears, the music was just a mess of notes. But occasionally, Ellen was able to extract shapes that formed an architectural mass. This was something Ellen excelled at; it was the essence of her musicality. She had an ability to carve out the music as if she was manipulating soft clay with precision, using a sharp knife, carefully balancing her movements, cutting away everything irrelevant, producing a fascinating but abstract three-dimensional artifact. What remained were the bare necessities; the composition opened up in a fragile, revealing light.

Very few persons realized this aspect of Ellen's talent. It was difficult to express in words. It was easier to express admiration for her dexterity, the beautiful tone or the emotion she conveyed. Mother understood. Ellen's teachers understood. The unknown benefactors who lent her a valuable Guarneri understood. Carola surmised it perhaps, but I never discussed it with her.

Ellen practiced so intensely during early fall that she didn't have time for anything else. She got permission to skip classes at school, woke up at six o'clock to get to an early practice session with her accompanist, she even skipped some meetings.

In September, she once went to one of the get-together parties for the congregation youth. Carola helped her get dressed up and clipped a small jewel onto her dress. Ellen stood in front of the mirror, pressed her lips together to spread the lipstick, and widened her eyes when she applied mascara. I mimicked her and pressed together my lips and widened my eyes. That was the last time we laughed together.

At the get-together, we didn't see each other much. The party was crowded. Ellen must have felt lonely because Barbara wasn't there anymore. I saw Ellen once in Timo's company, but after that, I lost sight of her. I should, of course, have kept an eye on her but I was only thinking about myself and about Paula.

Toward midnight, the party had moved forward to the next phase—chaos. Empty bottles, loud music, couples, third wheels who didn't know where to look or where to go.

I went out.

The evening was warm, some called it Indian summer. "When Will I Be Loved" boomed from the speakers.

Then I spotted Ellen. She was standing by the bushes in the dark. She had been drinking too much and she was crying and her dress was crumpled. I scolded myself because I had forgotten about her for several hours. The party was not over, but I decided to take her home.

Throughout that summer and early autumn, I had learned new things. I had a job at the Frenckell print shop, which had the most modern printing presses in the country. They had already stopped using relief printing several years earlier, changing to offset and computer-assisted photosetting. There I learned the basics of the printing industry, at first as an apprentice, later in more demanding roles. I was especially intrigued by the world of computers and noticed that even though I didn't have Carola's technical predisposition, it was easy to understand the cold logic of the computers. When Brother Weckman learned where I worked, he suggested that I could make use of what I had learned at the Finnish Branch Office and—the idea was fascinating—perhaps even in Brooklyn.

I was so excited about my new job that I initially didn't notice Ellen's transformation. One day, I became aware that she was playing apathetically and without having tuned the violin properly. I asked what was wrong, but she didn't respond. The following day she skipped a lesson, and then she stopped playing altogether. She withdrew into her shell, and we no longer had any connection with her. The change worried us; we tried to talk to her, we took her to a doctor.

The apple doesn't fall far from the tree, the brothers and sisters said as they watched her sit silently at the meetings. They nodded in sympathy and understanding, and there was no end to their knowledge.

Ellen recovered after a few weeks, but she had turned awfully silent. She used to explain things with precise, sometimes precocious expressions, but now she spoke slowly, meditatively, and I couldn't always understand what she meant. It was as if she was trying to tell me something but couldn't spell it out and just mixed hints and euphemisms into the conversation.

"Sometimes people disappoint you," she would say. "You think you know people and trust them."

It was as if she had sent an encrypted message on a secret frequency. I was worried that she was talking about me, but I didn't understand what she meant.

Or she would say "You would never stop talking to Carola, would you?"

"Why would I stop talking to her?"

She looked at me gravely. "Promise?"

I promised but wanted to know why.

"If something happens."

"Do you mean Simon Goldberg?"

"Such things happen easily. It's not always possible to do anything about it."

Sometimes we talked about Barbara. After being disfellow-shipped, she had moved to live with her aunt in Sweden and was living, so we were told, a depraved life. All who got disfellowshipped lived a depraved life, that was obvious. Ellen missed Barbara and felt lonely.

I said that we could take the ferry to Stockholm, we would find some credible pretext, and she would be able to meet Barbara in secret. We never got the opportunity to implement that idea.

We took long walks in Marjaniemi and in Tammisalo, but Ellen was no longer interested in fancy houses.

"Tell me about me," she said, as she had when we were little. It was as if we had regressed to being ten-years-olds again when I told her about wild gypsies, pirates, about the Romanian cargo ship, and she pretended to believe everything and asked for details, and I answered.

Ellen started playing again after a month, but from a competition point of view, it was too late. She had been accepted in the first round based on the tape recording she sent in, but her teacher decided to cancel. Ellen seemed not to care.

She cleaned her room, something she hardly ever did. She got rid of her old drawings and gave away toys that had become too childish, the Barbie dolls to Sofia and the stuffed animals to a neighbor.

She resumed her violin lessons, but her playing was reluctant, powerless.

Except for one time, just before she was hit by the train.

I had gone out but came back because it was cold outside and I wanted to take my cap. In the stairway, I could hear Ellen playing the first movement of Sibelius' Violin Concerto. I remained on the landing and listened.

This time, there was no sign of weakness or sluggishness. On the contrary, she performed the challenging concerto flawlessly, she played the fast sections with strength and fluency and above all, elasticity. The cadenza was brilliant. She began playing it slowly, almost contemplatively. She gradually increased the tempo and power and forced the violin to a furious final sprint.

I have never, neither before nor later, heard such a vital rendering of that concerto. I am sure that her version was more artistic than the performance of the Israeli violinist who later won the competition.

I didn't take my cap. When the music stopped and I could hear that Ellen had gone to the kitchen, I left. I wandered toward the shopping center. It was colder than usual in October, almost freezing. The crowd, the noise of the freeway, the noise from the excavator that worked on the metro construction project, and the concerto that still was ringing in my head got mixed together into a fabric that obscured my thoughts.

*

Ellen died a few days later. One frosty October morning, she was hit by a metro test train at the half-finished station in Kulosaari. We never got to know why she was in Kulosaari, or how she had ended up on the construction site at the station. She had brought the violin, but she wasn't on her way to a music lesson. The violin was found undamaged. The force of the collision had flung it towards the station, and it had landed on a bench next to the workers' tenements.

There is not much I can tell you about that fall. I do not remember. What I remember is just a haze. Sometimes I register small fragments of memories, but I don't know if they are something that I actually experienced or things that I imagine could have happened.

We mourned, but couldn't show it. We had to be strong, believe in the resurrection, show everyone that we had not been broken down.

I pulled away from the others. At work, I told no one about my sister's death. I couldn't stand the well-meaning pats on the shoulder, the turned-away eyes, the excessive consideration.

Several times each day, I got strange seizures that arrived in waves. My heart pounded and I shook and I felt physical pain in the stomach. The attacks lasted for half a minute and then returned. The seizures came unannounced, in the middle of a meal, at night, on the bus. Sometimes, they happened without any apparent reason, sometimes they occurred when I ran into something that had belonged to her. A pencil she used when she marked her notes, a lost hairclip that waited to be discovered in the slit between the sofa cushions. When

I smelled resin or saw a garment in the particular color that Ellen liked, the dark green hue of pine needles.

I tried not to think of her, and after some time I succeeded. I immersed myself in my work for hours and sometimes forgot about the surrounding world.

In November, when the first slippery weather occurred, I fell as I ran to the bus and the asphalt tore bleeding scrapes on my knee and both hands. I continued without stopping. The physical pain was easy to endure, and I noticed that I could reduce the pain by watering it down, adding more pain until I felt nothing.

In January, it had been three months since Ellen's death. We arranged the get-together party at Bellevue; our intention was to demonstrate that we were firm in our faith and that life could continue.

I already told you about this event.

After Timo Auramo's death, the get-togethers were prohibited. I was already working at the Branch Office in Tikkurila, but I still lived at home as there were no available rooms in the accommodation building.

I don't know when Carola started thinking about leaving our faith. It was not a case of a dramatic conflict or a sudden insight. But the life we lived was not a life she wanted to live. Maybe she had immediately regretted getting baptized.

Half a year after Ellen's death the pattern became more visible. Carola fabricated excuses to avoid going to the meetings. Headaches, late working hours, unspecified urgent matters. She completely stopped doing field service.

In May, she was called to a judicial committee meeting. Someone had seen her with Simon Goldberg.

We were sitting in a café at the Boulevard because these were things you couldn't discuss at home. Carola ordered a café au lait, but the waitress didn't know what she meant, so she had to settle for cold milk in her coffee.

"I'm not going to take part in that charade," she said.

"You don't have a choice," I said.

"I can choose not to go. I know very well what they will ask. Have you seen each other naked? Have you touched each other, where, for how long, was it *porneia*, loose conduct or unclean behavior? They will read Bible verses and excerpts from the magazine, and they will pray. I will have to tell all the details and cry a little to show remorse, and they will want to know if I regret the sin or the penalty. They will read something from the secret handbook for elders and then give judgment."

She opened her bag.

A passport. Cash. A ticket to Stockholm on Viking Line.

"Paris," she said.

"You'll be disfellowshipped," I said, more as an observation than as a warning.

The morning before the scheduled hearing, she disappeared. She woke up early, packed her scarce belongings, took the morning bus to Turku, the day ferry to Stockholm, and the night train to Copenhagen.

I told no one what I knew about her plans, but from the very beginning, it was clear to everyone that she had disappeared of her own will. At her job, they told us that she had resigned on short notice. Her bank account was drained. Her small suitcase was gone.

Three weeks later, we received a postcard from Paris. It was only a short greeting, no explanation. When Father came home and saw the postcard, he tore it in half.

On the stage, they announced that Carola was disfellow-shipped. My parents sat motionless in their seats and stared straight ahead. Father was red-faced, Mother was pale. A week later, there was a talk about the perils young people run into when they seek bad company. Father lost his privileges.

Neither Father, Mother nor Sofia ever spoke to Carola again. For them, she was worse than a worldly person. Disfellowshipped, an apostate, an evil person. Father requested that Carola's name never be mentioned in our home again. He said that it would have been better if she was dead. I suspect that he wasn't proud of this, that he was secretly ashamed of his cowardice. Carola told me later that he sent her a letter and justified himself at length, citing the magazine and the Flock book. He wrote that he had no choice, that it was not easy for him to renounce his own child, that there was nothing he wished more than that she would repent and come back.

I kept my promise to Ellen. I stayed in touch with Carola. I didn't even bother to keep it a secret. As long as I didn't openly advertise that I socialized with a disfellowshipped relative, nobody cared. There were some advantages to being part of the Brooklyn elite.

Carola told me that she once happened to meet our father and Sofia on the street. They looked right through her. Another time, she waited outside the Kingdom Hall to see a glimpse of him and Mother. Many years later, when she was already married, she called the Branch Office to get her baptism canceled. Her husband Rolf had figured out that because shunning would not apply to persons who weren't baptized, she just had to get the baptism canceled based on some technicality: she was a minor, not in the position to take such a decision, or temporarily unstable. Or something. It was, of course, not possible to cancel the baptism. When she had her son Max, our father sent her a letter stating he would like to learn to know Max, although he still could not have anything to do with Carola herself. Carola wrote back that, in that case, he was not the kind of man she wanted in her son's life. Only twice had Carola met any other relative than me: at Mother's funeral and recently, at Sofia's.

I sometimes think about Ellen's final weeks and the events of the following winter. Over the years, I have tried to talk to Carola about all this, about Ellen kissing her reflection, her music, her death, about the get-together parties, about Timo Auramo, the ice and Bellevue. But we found no words, they seemed trivial. If we said something, we said it in a low voice.

Some things are so difficult to touch that it is better to pretend that time heals all wounds.

Part IV

Ruby

28

In mid-April, everything changed. First, Ron Miller wanted to arrange the vote, then Sofia died, and I received the letter from the woman who claimed to be my daughter.

Miller and I were at our weekly meeting.

After persuading Derrick to give up the idea of transferring the Warwick project to Patrick O'Hare, I spent all my energy, all my life to get the construction started. We had negotiated with the county and the neighbors for a long time, countless plans had been put forward and rejected, but finally, we got our building permit. The project stayed on schedule, the annex buildings were almost finished, and the framework for the main building was being erected. I had adapted my father's method to a larger scale, and I planned to invite him to the inauguration. We had already decided on the exact day we would move in.

But because of the economy, it was difficult to sell our properties in Brooklyn, and therefore the financing was not yet secured. The economy of the organization was weak; the first quarter was the worst in decades. Our day-to-day administration was too massive, and we hadn't been able to save enough by cutting a little here, a little there. We needed structural changes. I had already considered discontinuing or postponing all other construction projects except for Warwick.

But these were operational technicalities, and they bored Miller. He had reached the age of eighty and such things he delegated to others.

Nowadays he was interested only in his reformation program, of which he had already completed a few parts.

"Bad news," I said.

"Let's hear it," Miller said.

"There are too many voters that we don't control. Some people we are sure of, but Baldwin is undecided. There are at least two or three others who are waiting for his assessment."

Miller's worst competitor was the coordinator of the Writing Committee, Alan Shayne. He had become a burden. He was old school, and his ideas were not really up-to-date. But since he headed the Writing Committee, he more or less controlled the contents of books and magazines, and this caused confusion and concern. Miller wanted to get rid of Alan Shayne. Shayne could, in principle, be appointed to some token management position outside the Governing Body, but there was a risk that through the back door he could wield greater influence than he rightly deserved. Miller wanted to keep Shayne in Governing Body but curtailed in his powers. Shayne wouldn't give up his position without a fight, so we needed the support of the others in GB. And we had to offer something in exchange.

It would have been possible to adjust the contents of the portfolios, for example, so that the Personnel Committee and the Publishing Committee would have a single coordinator and the portfolio thus would seem more enticing. Not everybody would accept such a change because it would mean that somebody else lost a position. As a counterweight, it was necessary to give one or two positions to people who were neutral. For months, we had tried to find a solution.

That's why Miller devised an original solution. By pushing a vote on some controversial doctrine, he could to force everyone in the Governing Body to take a stand. It was, of course, essential to choose the right issue. We had been discussing the doctrine of the Trinity, our teaching about blood and the Generation doctrine. We had discussed possible scenarios and made a risk assessment. The Trinity doctrine would have been the easiest to change, from a technical point of view. The word "trinity" did not exist in the Bible, so we needed no new translation, only rewrite our interpretations. But strategically, it would have been a high-risk option. The Generation doctrine we had already changed twice, so Miller didn't think that was a viable alternative.

Finally, Miller decided on changing our teaching about blood.

This was one of our most sacred teachings. It banned all use of blood, including for medical use. It was one of the most fundamental teachings and separated us from the Catholics. Shayne would, of course, oppose any change, but if the majority voted in favor, Shayne had to give up, and Miller would get rid of his rival.

We designed the proposal together. Initially, the proposal was radical, but when we discovered how much some people opposed it, we softened the positions, extended transition periods and included in the package something that Shayne and his followers wanted: a stricter attitude toward shunning former members. But the situation was so even that we couldn't be sure of the outcome.

James Baldwin could tip the balance. We had counted on him, but now he had got cold feet. His followers mostly voted with him. Now Baldwin had decided that this was a matter of conscience, and he seemed to be leaning towards voting against our suggestion.

Miller rolled his wheelchair to the window. He spoke to me but looked at the New York skyline.

"Baldwin is your responsibility, Markus. I want you to create a package that makes sure we win. I'll give you carte blanche. Do what you have to do, but make sure you get his support."

"Okay," I said. "I'll ensure it."

"Markus, 'ensure' sounds as if you are going to make sure that someone else does it. You will not ensure. You will execute."

I nodded. I had to promise Baldwin something, but that was a trap that he would fall into because of his greed. When everything was said and done, Baldwin would realize that he had been outplayed. This was how Miller treated small fry.

Miller turned his wheelchair toward me.

"How long have you been living in the US? For thirty years, longer even. There's something about you. You get people to listen to you, even if they don't agree with you. Some people are afraid of you, you command respect, and that's valuable in this industry. You are popular on both sides. Do you have any idea what kind of power you could have if you just exercised it right?"

I shrugged. I executed, but I was no politician. I was mostly considered neutral, although I obviously was known to support Miller.

"But here's something for you to chew on. If we win the vote, Alan Shayne is basically gone, and we can make a few changes to the Governing Body. Guess who then becomes the coordinator of the Writing Committee?"

I mentioned a few names. The coordinator of Australia was in line for a position in the Governing Body. On the other hand, it might be sensible from an equal opportunity point of view to appoint an African-American.

He looked at me for a moment.

"We will appoint you. Markus Gunnarson Douglas."

I never saw that coming. I admit that I had been toying with the idea of being a member of the Governing Body, but only in maybe ten or twenty years. And certainly not in any important position. Now Miller suggested that I would be appointed directly to the Writing Committee.

If Miller's plan worked out, I would be one of the youngest members of the Governing Body ever. The problem was that, by allowing me to get one of the most powerful portfolios, they would sidestep some older brothers who had patiently waited for their turn. To ignore the old foxes and promote a relatively young European was risky.

This was a declaration of war.

"I'm a manager," I said, hoping I sounded humble enough. "I've controlled economic and organizational planning. I have organized assemblies. Construction projects and speaker tours. Process development. I'm hardly the right man to lead the Writing Committee."

"You can write. Unlike many others who have led the Writing Committee."

"The Writing Committee isn't a position for someone who can write, it's a position for a chief ideologue."

"You'll have the full support of the GB."

We fell silent for a while.

"But of course you'll have to loosen your grip on Warwick."

At first, I wanted to protest, but suddenly I saw the crystal-clear logic. Warwick was the tip of the iceberg. This wasn't about the property or about me, it was about getting the support from Baldwin and from the real estate department. Miller would win the vote and could get rid of his adversary. Out of pure gratitude, I would vote with Miller on all important issues, and he would in practice have power over everything that was written. With me on the Writing Committee and his competitor outwitted, Miller would have control over the entire ninth floor.

"Trust me. I know where I can get hold of Baldwin tonight," I said.

"In Halcyon," Miller said.

I wasn't surprised that Miller knew. He wasn't a member of Halcyon, but on the ninth floor, they knew everything.

58 Joralemon Street looked the same as the other buildings around. It was a three-story brownstone, and there were no signs or posters. There was nothing that would have made a random observer believe that it wasn't just an ordinary residential building. When I lived around the corner on Willow Place, I knew nothing about the Halcyon society and never noticed that inconspicuous house.

If you looked closely at the building, you could see that the windows weren't made of glass but of dark, opaque polycarbonate. You couldn't look out from the inside, but more importantly, it was impossible to look in from the outside.

I arrived at precisely the allotted time. We had our personal arrival times and routes because we didn't want the neighbors to notice the flow of visitors. I rang the doorbell, three short signals, our code. The door phone woke up, there was a low murmur, and a male voice asked how he could help me.

"*Denmark*. Eight forty, Douglas, one."

There was a buzz, and I entered.

This day my arrival time was among the last, and the party had already begun. People were moving between floors. In the dining room, you could hear clinks of cutlery. The largest hall was still empty. At this hour, the activities took place in the smaller rooms on the second and third floor. Everywhere you could hear faint music through loudspeakers hidden in the wall. It was vague, non-melodic synthesizer music, oddly distorted, as if the speakers were submerged in water.

I took a glass of champagne served on a silver platter by a bare-breasted girl. I really didn't want any champagne, but I liked to have something in my hand; it permitted me to go around, looking, without being forced to take part. Glass in my hand, I went upstairs.

The Halcyon building was built on a narrow plot of land. Five floors, three aboveground and two below. On the ground floor, there was an alarmed emergency exit. It led to a service tunnel for the subway, and you could reach the Borough Hall station through it. Originally the house was built around the subway's ventilation shaft, and therefore the house was labyrinthic and obscure. Whenever a train passed under the house, you could hear a low rumble, bottles and glasses rattling on shelves, and after a moment a loud swooshing from the ventilation duct.

People were moving in both directions in the stairs between the floors, searching for a suitable room to watch or to participate. Most were dressed according to the dress code, in tuxedos or evening gowns. Some women's dresses were cut so that they covered the throat but left the breasts exposed. The men's costumes were mostly conservative, but occasionally you could glimpse leather or latex.

On the landing on the second floor, I could hear noises from the rooms, overriding the subdued music. Heavy breathing, moans, sighs, quiet sounds of pain or pleasure, comical slapping when flesh bumped against flesh. It was dark inside the rooms, but when my eyes adapted to the darkness, I could see shadows lying on top of each other or relaxed in each other's arms.

In Halcyon, everything was permitted, nothing was mandatory.

For a while, I watched the activities going on in the rooms. The movements and expressions of pleasure felt learned. They seemed intended for the other participants and the spectators, as if everything was about to get recorded on tape. It was okay to watch, but it was better not to show too much interest. You could join a couple if you wanted to, but usually, some kind of invitation was expected, a small movement of a hand, or a wink.

I recognized many faces and also knew some names. There were no important or less important members. We were all equals, and we only used our first names. Outside these premises, we never referred to Halcyon. What happened in Halcyon, stayed in Halcyon.

In the third room, two men were watching the activities. They conversed intensely, heads together, in low voices. One of the men was Baldwin.

I had to wait for some time before Baldwin was alone so that I could talk to him one-on-one. We walked down the narrow stairs to the ground floor where the main hall was still being prepared. The mattresses were in place, but the light was bright, as if in preparation for cleaning. Within half an hour, everything would be ready. We continued down to the spa in the basement. There was a heated swimming pool, showers and some sort of chamber called a sauna. It was merely a small warm room that had sauna benches but no visible stove. There used to be a Swedish sauna heater in there, but the combination of water and electricity was considered lethal, and the heater unit was removed. Now, the room was heated with a standard radiator, and the temperature never rose above 120 F.

We were alone in the spa. The sauna was a safe place for conversation. We stripped, Baldwin swam a few laps in the pool, and then we relaxed with our towels around the hips in the sauna.

I brought up the vote. Baldwin said that he couldn't possibly give in on the blood issue. If we changed the policy now, it would lead to an outcry.

I explained that we already had changed the policy. "We already have pushed the envelope. We allow white blood cells and plasma. It's just about removing the boundaries altogether."

According to the proposal, it still wouldn't be permissible to eat blood, but we would allow blood transfusions. First, we would make it a matter of conscience, then we would recommend that you should not cause others to stumble by refusing a transfusion, and eventually we would able to forget the whole thing. I said that this was consistent with previous changes.

"We have renewed our organization, we are using state-of-the-art printing technology, our management processes are quality-certified. We are building new office spaces. But our image is from the fifties and our teachings from the nineteenth century."

Baldwin said it was a matter of principle.

"We have already watered down the Generation doctrine," he said and pointed out that we had also reduced the requirements for meetings and field service. We had discontinued publications and adjusted the doctrines so that they were easier to accept. "Where should we stop? Should we embrace the doctrine of the Trinity? Should we appoint women to be elders?"

I said it was a fact that blood transfusions in due course would be accepted. If we lost the vote now, hundreds of people would die needlessly.

"I know why Miller wants this vote," Baldwin snorted. "He wants to smoke Shayne out of his trench."

Baldwin was not stupid, though he didn't see the full picture.

Two young women stepped down the stairs. The blonde one I recognized but the brunette was new. In principle, only married couples were allowed, but in practice, many men came alone, so there was always a shortage of women. Therefore the Halcyon board had invited reliable and attractive young women. This new one seemed gentle and shy. She looked like somebody's daughter.

The women undressed and felt the water with their feet. When they saw us, they made a questioning gesture. I lifted a hand to show that we wanted to be left alone. They shrugged and slid into the water.

"Do you know, Markus, what miners used to do to ensure that the air was breathable?" Baldwin asked and continued without waiting for an answer: "They had a canary. If the bird died, the air was toxic or depleted of oxygen. I'm not going to be the canary in this matter. I'll vote no."

Baldwin got up and opened the sauna door. The girls in the pool smiled at him.

Ron Miller expected results.

"Kingdom Support Services," I said.

Baldwin stopped in the doorway. He turned his eyes toward me.

"We'll have to reorganize. Your name came up."

"Please elaborate."

"Someone has to take charge of Kingdom Support Services. If you support us, Miller will appoint you."

Baldwin was silent for a minute.

"I don't trust Miller. I want that in writing."

When we went back up, the atmosphere was electrified. The lights were dimmed, and you could see naked people everywhere moving between the floors.

This was the core of the Halcyon society. Alcohol, sweets, marijuana and other superficial vices only brought temporary pleasure, not sufficient to offset the long-term side effects. Sex was beneficial for the heart and warmed the soul, and was now practically harmless. In principle, everyone could enjoy it without fear of consequences. Therefore, it was forbidden and something that needed to be controlled.

I stayed for a while because I didn't want to be the first one to leave. I had heard that the parties sometimes deteriorated in the wee hours, but I never stayed long enough to find out what deteriorated meant. Recently, I had noticed that I often wanted to go home early, and sometimes I found excuses not to go at all. The parties were exciting in the early evening, but permission reduces the appeal of the forbidden.

At midnight, I went home.

I filled my lungs with the crisp, fresh night air.

I turned on to Henry Street. I walked briskly and glanced at my phone.

Three missed calls. There was a short message on my answering machine. Sofia was dead.

29

It was already late when Carola and I left the restaurant and walked back toward the hotel. It was a cloud-free night, but due to the lights, we couldn't see many stars in the April sky. I could see a few spots here and there, and a bright light in the west—a star or a planet. Nautical twilight. I couldn't remember whether Venus should appear in the morning or in the evening.

I mentioned the forthcoming changes in the management team.

"In the past, during Roman times, decimation was a way of punishment," Carola said. "When they couldn't punish the entire regiment, they picked one out of ten to be executed. Some commercial companies nowadays are also using decimation. Every year they fire the lowest performing ten percent and hire new ones instead. Perhaps you are also culling."

"Don't worry, I can stand up for myself."

"I'm not worried about you, you're a man. I'm thinking of women and children; they will always suffer when men compete. In war, politics, religion."

We had arrived at the market square. We stopped and looked out over the sea.

"Do you remember," Carola said, "when we were young and believed that all evil in the world existed because a naked woman accepted a fruit from a talking snake? That the entire world would be destroyed in a few years? That there would be a paradise instead and only the preachers of the word would survive? Do you still believe in that? That it is the truth?"

I shrugged.

"Even if it turns out that this is not the truth, this is a good way to live."

"A good way to live? I respect your right to control your own life, but are you truly living the life you want? I believe that this is the only life we have, and that's why we must seize it. I know you see it differently, but when you look back on your life, don't you regret anything?"

I was silent for a moment. We rarely spoke of private things; we pushed the emotional and profound discussions aside.

"I do regret that I left Alison. If I had stayed with her, everything would be different."

Carola chuckled.

I wanted her to understand. "I still love Alison. She is the only woman I've ever loved. And she is probably the only one who ever loved me."

"Markus, you're in love with a ghost. You don't love her. You only ever loved yourself. And she didn't love you, she loved the one she thought you were."

I assumed a hurt expression.

"Sometimes you are such a jerk."

"I'm sorry. I'm just allergic to people who deceive themselves."

*

Carola was right, of course. I didn't love Alison. I couldn't recall the feeling of being in love. At an abstract level, I knew how it should feel, but couldn't evoke the emotion. It was as if I remembered the punch line of a joke, but didn't think it was funny anymore. What I felt wasn't love. But I didn't know what word to choose. Is there a word for what you feel for someone you have loved but no longer love?

The word "love" has lost its meaning and has become a lazy standard expression for something you don't care to articulate with precision. We love objects with the same word we love life, people with the same word as food. In Greek, there were many different words: *agápē, érōs, philía*. Love of God, the love between man and woman, the bond between friends. And, above all, *storgē*, love within the family. Between siblings, between a child and a parent.

It wasn't true that I only had loved myself. I thought about my family, my parents, Carola, Ellen, Sofia.

And about my unknown daughter.

I didn't tell Carola about the letter I had received. I knew very well who sent the letter. Before I followed Chris Huebinger's advice, I had been with only one woman other than Debra. Either this Ellen Leblanc was an impostor who, for some obscure reason wanted to infiltrate my life, or she was Alison's daughter.

30

Sometimes somebody you believe is your friend is just some-one who finds you useful, a means to an end. You see it clearly when the utility aspect is gone and you no longer have a com-mon goal.

While I was sitting on the plane on my way back to New York, Ron Miller pulled his proposal. Something had hap-pened, perhaps Baldwin had lied to me, and maybe his group wouldn't have voted in favor.

Miller didn't want to take the risk. Instead, he and Baldwin had agreed on a new organization model, where everything that had to do with properties was taken away from me and transferred to the real estate department. The Kingdom Sup-port Services had been assigned to Baldwin. I was, of course, not nominated for a position in the Governing Body.

Miller didn't explain himself, but he suggested that I take some time off.

"You know that the organization is facing great challenges. The situation is inflamed, and you have been identified as an opponent of the current strategy, with or without reason. Take some time off, rest a little. Go see your wife in California."

I said that I didn't need to rest.

At first, I couldn't interpret Miller's expression. It was as if I saw a staged photography shoot where the person depicted was aware of the camera and only pretended to do something.

I understood. The canary.

"You never intended to have a vote on the blood doctrine. You just wanted to get Baldwin into your own camp. You sacrificed me."

He still said nothing. We looked at each other and both knew that the other knew.

It took some time before I contacted Ellen Leblanc. I was in Finland the day she had proposed a meeting, and the first week after my trip I spent in dealing with the aftermath of the organizational change.

A couple of times I had the phone in my hand and intended to call the number, but I didn't. Her surname bothered me, it sounded familiar. But I didn't know any Leblanc.

I went to the reception to ask.

"It was a young woman. She didn't seem to be one of us," the brother said and tried to remember. It had already been two weeks.

"She seemed more like some kind of artist or hipster or bum."

I walked home. At the station, a girl who looked like a hip-hopper stared in front of her and muttered, "Rape Me." I assumed that she only stated the name of the song she was listening to through her headphones.

I switched to the other side of the street, where there was a bookstore.

When I walked past the bookstore, I suddenly understood why the name Ellen Leblanc sounded familiar. Ellen Leblanc was a Canadian author who wrote in English. Her debut novel had attracted attention a few years back. I hadn't read it, but now that I saw the stacks of books and the posters in the window of Barnes & Noble, I remembered her name.

I stepped into the bookstore. It was a small shop, but since the novel had been on *The New York Times* best-seller list, it should still be available. It was. When I mentioned the name, the helpful clerk led me to the correct shelf and handed me the book.

Outside, I flipped through the book. It was called *The Lady of the Lake*, and it seemed to be a love story with a background in a dysfunctional family. There was no photograph of the author on the cover.

At home, I did a search online. The search engine knew thousands of references to people named Ellen Leblanc. I found both photographs and video clips. The name wasn't exactly unusual, but most of the links led to information about Ellen Leblanc, the author.

I studied photographs of her. She was in her thirties, blonde and tall.

It is easy to imagine similarities when you are searching for them. We see what we want to see.

The eyes, maybe. The cheekbones, perhaps.

I clicked on a video clip taken at a book fair.

Ellen Leblanc read a passage from her book and then answered the interviewer's questions. The video was amateurish, most likely taken with a cell phone, and the sound was distorted and of such low quality that I could not always discern the words. But there was no doubt about it, I knew that voice.

It was Alison's voice.

It was Alison's inflection.

Alison's gestures, Alison's way of raising up her chin.

The year of birth matched. Now her looks also matched.

Ellen Leblanc resembled her mother, but she was taller, more a model than a country girl. When I looked more closely at the images, I noticed that Ellen Leblanc had my nose, a Douglas nose, and my lips. The eyes were undeniably Alison's. I saw a glimpse of Carola in the narrow face.

According to Wikipedia, Ellen Leblanc was born in Rochester, New York and raised in Trois-Rivières, Quebec. Her mother was Alison Killarney, and the father was unknown. When Ellen was twelve months old, her mother moved to Canada and married a French Canadian. Ellen Leblanc was bilingual, held dual citizenship, and currently lived in Brooklyn. *The Lady of the Lake* was her debut novel and had sold over 100,000 copies. A movie based on it was about to be filmed.

I read the novel that night. It was a well-written love story, and I understood why it had attracted attention. I tried to find some references to Alison, or to myself—the absent father—but while many debut novels are about the writer's family and her own coming-of-age, I saw no clear indicators.

I programmed Ellen Leblanc's number into my phone, but every time I was about to call her, I put it off. I always found a reason not to call. In the morning you couldn't call, because artists slept in. During lunchtime, you couldn't call, she'd be eating. In the afternoon she'd be working, and in the evening the child is asleep.

*

Then I had to forget about Ellen Leblanc for a time because the coordinator of the Personnel Committee asked for a meeting.

His door was ajar. I knocked once and stepped in. He had a phone conversation going on, but I got the impression that there was no-one on the line. He pressed the phone to his ear with his shoulder and used both hands to browse through his papers as he spoke. The intention was to make an impression of a busy man on top of everything. He raised his head and saw me, but continued to talk. He paused as if listening to the other party and made an apologetic gesture, tapped on his watch and moved his lips, *three minutes, okay?*

I studied his room. It was bigger than mine, but the view was to the north. On the table, he had a clichéd picture of the leaning tower of Pisa. Somebody was standing in the foreground, holding his hand so that it looked as if he was supporting the tower. But the illusion didn't work, because there was air between the hand and the tower. But maybe this was intentional. If so, the picture was not ridiculous tourist junk but an ironic comment on that kind of tourist junk. But I suspected that the photo was just ineptly taken.

He finished his conversation.

"Markus, I'll cut to the chase. Our resource needs have changed, and we have decided to reallocate our assets. I think it would be better for you if you no longer had to be bound by the obligations of a position at the headquarters. We'll arrange a start-up grant to help you adjust to the new situation."

"Excuse me?" I pondered for a moment. "Are you firing me?"

"This is not about being fired. It's about matching supply and demand. We want to give you the opportunity to seek new challenges."

I never give anybody the finger or use expletives. I simply left.

My father used to say that if you piss in the snow, there will be a hole. I should have seen the signs, they had been fully visible.

Sometimes when I stepped into the break room, the talking stopped. More often than not, I found myself having lunch alone. Most of my colleagues were friendly, some even overly friendly, but certain brothers looked straight through me when we met in the corridors. I was not invited to planning meetings. The coordination group spent a weekend at Lake Placid, but I didn't hear about it until later. I only made the connection when I backtracked and examined the events the way you review the accounts after bankruptcy.

The following day, Baldwin called me.

"Brother Douglas," he said. "Your name has come up, and I hope that we could have a discussion."

Brother Douglas, not Markus. Your name has come up. A discussion.

I knew what it meant.

There were four. I nodded to them, and we didn't shake hands. Baldwin was the chairman, the others I only knew in passing. They were committee or department secretaries or middle management. Ron Miller wasn't there.

The meeting room was the smaller conference room in the east wing. It was suitable for one-on-ones or small groups. In this room, I had countless times discussed organizational changes with Miller, negotiated contracts with lawyers, spread out blueprints and cost estimates with property managers.

On the wall was an organizational chart from an earlier session, with pictures of members of the Governing Body and the chairmen of the coordination groups, and there were red arrows and yellow post-it notes between them. There was no photograph of me.

From the window, I could see the Brooklyn Bridge and the Manhattan Bridge and the East River. The Manhattan skyline. Far away, a plane was about to land at LaGuardia.

Baldwin had a bunch of papers in front of him. I would have smiled at this childish way to create artificial authority, but the nature of the meeting didn't encourage amusement.

He explained that the goal of the meeting was just to have a chat. There had been accusations, and they wanted to investigate their truthfulness.

"If I'm accused of something, I want to know who is accusing," I said.

"We don't really care what you want," said the brother who sat next to me.

"Do you care what the Bible says? If someone wants to bring a charge against a brother, he should first discuss the matter in private."

Baldwin assumed the role of mediator.

"You're right, but in this case, I don't think it'll be necessary or even feasible."

He browsed through his papers and assumed a troubled expression before he continued.

"Your sister Sofia Tanner died in April this year. We are sorry for your loss."

"Thank you. We were close, even though we were living on different continents."

"The funeral was in the middle of April, right?"

I nodded. They knew very well when the funeral took place; it was a day before the extraordinary meeting of the Governing Body.

"You traveled there to attend, of course. Did you take the opportunity to meet relatives too?"

"Of course. I don't go to Finland that often. It's been more than ten years since the last time."

"You also have another sister, Carola Douglas. Did she attend the funeral?"

"Of course. And yes, it is true that she is disfellowshipped."

"There is no objection to meeting disfellowshipped relatives when there are important family matters to discuss. But you met her again after the funeral, right?"

"True. We hadn't met for a long time, and there was a lot to talk about."

"I understand. Inheritance and so forth. But you have also been seen in a restaurant."

I realized what this would lead to.

"And the timing was pretty strange for a family conversation. It was nine o'clock in the evening."

"You can't be serious. Sure, we had dinner together."

"And what was the name of the restaurant?"

"How would I remember something like that? It was an Italian restaurant, in the center of Helsinki."

"La Famíglia?"

"Possibly. Probably."

Baldwin smiled victoriously.

"An appropriate name, easy to remember in this case. No need to trouble our witness. You admit that you had dinner with your sister in the restaurant La Famíglia in Helsinki, on April nineteenth this year."

He said it as if it was a statement that would be recorded in the protocol.

He opened his Bible.

"I'm sure you are aware of the principles guiding what kind of people we should associate with. You have admitted that you had dinner with a disfellowshipped person. The Bible makes no concessions on this point. 'You should not even eat with them.' What do you think the brothers and sisters would think if this came out?"

"This is absurd, and you know it. Firstly, we had important family matters to discuss. Secondly, she is my sister."

"Brother Douglas, we are not here to judge you but to sort out the truth about the allegations that have been made. You have committed a serious misstep."

He was silent for a moment.

"But there is a solution."

I said nothing. The personnel coordinator had already told me about the solution.

"Given your long history and your obvious willingness to continue to be a part of this organization, we will try and find a compromise, an agreement that would let you get honorably out of this."

"You want me to admit that I made a mistake? Okay, I admit that I broke the printed rules of the organization about eating a with a disfellowshipped person. Is that good enough?"

"Your attitude is not constructive."

"You are accusing me of having had dinner with my sister."

They looked at each other. This was something they had discussed in advance, and the result was what they had expected.

"Thank you, Brother Douglas. The meeting has achieved its purpose."

I went directly into Ron Miller's office. He knew, of course, what was going on and had been waiting for me. I remained standing, and he rolled his wheelchair to his table.

"Your time at the headquarters is over," he said. "This has already gone too far, and I don't want to continue like this. You only have this one chance, there won't be another one. You will resign immediately. Take your severance pay and go wherever you want. There will be no judicial committee because your indiscretion is not widely known. You will have a clean record to bring to the congregation of your choice. But you must resign now."

"And if I refuse?"

"In that case, you'll have to take your chances with a judicial committee. And after a committee hearing, you'll be marked, even if you get away with no conviction. And you will most certainly be convicted. If your attitude is not considered to show sincere repentance, you will be disfellowshipped."

He put his mechanical toy in motion. Miller was like the sphere in the middle; nothing affected him, he just channeled the energy until something happened at the other end.

"Ron," I said. "Do you remember a long time ago, when you visited Finland? You gave a talk at an assembly."

"Yes?"

"You saw a young girl who played the violin and you exchanged a few words with her brother."

"I've been to Helsinki once. It is possible that I remember something like that. Why?"

"The girl was my sister. That boy was me."

Miller stared at me without saying a word. Something in his eyes clicked into place.

"It was you."

"You were my hero. I admired you. I have supported you all these years. I thought you were my friend."

"Markus, I am your friend. It's possible that I'm your only friend. If you want a friend who is trying to please you, get a dog. You agreed to give up the construction project in exchange for a position on the Governing Body. You wanted to be one of the big boys. It was not enough for you that you got all the women you could imagine, the membership of the Halcyon, your office on the eighth floor, your stadium appearances, your M&M candies sorted according to color. That wasn't enough for you. You thought that you could go even further, but this is a game for the big players."

"I don't deserve to be treated like this."

Miller pointed to a photograph on the table. The picture was of himself as a zealous young brother, in his twenties.

"When I started, I was nobody. An errand boy. I got to clean Brother K. H. Norrman's toilet. I built up my position myself. If something goes wrong, I look in the mirror, I don't blame the economy or the weather or the government. You can't tell me what I can or cannot do. When you came to Brooklyn, you were nobody. Everything you have achieved is because of me. You are capable, one of the best. But your time is up. Go grab a beer. Go fuck a trolley dolly. Don't take it personally."

"After all these years, after everything we have been through together, you are prepared to have me disfellowshipped for having dinner at a restaurant with my sister?"

"I can have you disfellowshipped for anything I want, it doesn't matter. It has happened before, you know that. And you can't seriously claim that you don't deserve to be disfellowshipped. All these women, the Halcyon society. Don't be a hypocrite."

"I could bring many brothers down with me."

"True. But you can only bring down those who we want to get rid of anyway."

He took a paper from a drawer and examined it for a moment, as if trying to give the impression that he was seeing it for the first time. He pushed the paper over to me. It was the letter of resignation I had signed when I started. It had been archived all these years, waiting for this moment. I just had to fill in the date.

A pair of young brothers followed me to my office to seize my computer. They had walkie-talkies fastened on the shoulders, making them look like security goons.

"I have personal documents on that computer. I want to transfer them to a memory stick before you take it."

"Unfortunately, we cannot allow that. If there is something that you need, you will get it later, after the security department has gone through it. Standard procedure."

I returned my phone, my badge, and my keys. I signed a form stating that any travel expenses and other overhead costs that the organization still owed me were included in the severance compensation. I packed my possessions into a plastic bag.

I got the severance money in cash.

It dawned on me that this had been prepared before I even knew what was going on. The girl at the cash register must have gone to the bank early in the morning to withdraw cash. She counted the notes into my hand without looking me in the eyes. The two goons escorted me out.

31

The first time I met my daughter Ellen Leblanc was at the Starbucks at Franklin Avenue. We sat opposite each other; she had a latte in front of her, I had an espresso. Her little daughter was quiet during the short meeting and stared at me with her big eyes.

I don't know what I had expected, perhaps a romantic movie scene, strings in the background, a harp glissando, father and daughter, the first encounter. Maybe I thought that we would instantly feel a deep affinity, that we would note that we had the same kind of humor, and were interested in the same odd things. Maybe we both liked our coffee black and strong, perhaps we both preferred open landscapes and proximity to the sea.

I did try.

I wanted to get to know her, but she didn't let me get close. I asked questions, she answered them as if I were a salesman at a department store, in an impersonal, neutral voice.

We kept to safe waters. I told her about my trips and my job. She told me about her studies, her daughter, her book. When I said I had read it, she asked some seemingly innocent questions about it, but I knew that she was testing me. I didn't take offense. Maybe she was pleased that I had read it and actually understood the details she hadn't spelled out, but if so, she didn't show it.

There was an unwritten agreement between us, that we would keep to subjects she chose. Therefore I asked nothing about Alison, and she told me nothing of her own accord. She said that she had always known my name and where she could find me.

We met again, in a park.

The third time we met we walked over the Brooklyn Bridge to Manhattan. She was still indifferent, covertly but discernibly hostile.

I wasn't sure I liked her, this woman who was my daughter.

But her little girl, Ruby, stole my heart.

Ruby was strikingly reminiscent of my kid sister Ellen, not so much in appearance as in her forthright, lively, somewhat precocious way. Ruby was verbally developed and in a phase when she asked loads of questions. The timid silence from our first meeting was gone and now she was constantly chatting. She wanted to know everybody's name, even the names of strangers she saw on the street or people on advertising posters. She wanted to know the breed and names of all the dogs we met, and what they liked to eat. She wanted to know where the water in the river came from and why it didn't stay where it was. Sometimes I had to admit to her that I didn't know everything.

I threw her high up in the air and she screamed in terror and delight. I distorted my face and growled and pretended to be dangerous and she pretended to be scared and ran away screaming, but when I stopped she immediately came back and wanted to play again.

I read aloud to her, and she listened as intently as my little sister Ellen used to do.

I knew nothing about Ruby's father. The agreement between Ellen and me stipulated that I did not ask.

Once, when Ellen casually mentioned Alison, I noticed that she said "was" instead of "is". I looked at her questioningly and she got annoyed.

"If you had wanted to contact my mother, it would have been rather easy to find her. If she had wanted to contact you, she would have known where to go. So don't you say anything, you know nothing. You made your choice, you have no right to know, you've forfeited that right."

She put Ruby in her stroller, turned around and walked back home. Ruby peeked out around her mother and waved to me.

I couldn't blame Ellen. The only thing I could do was to open up myself and invite her into my world, and hope that at some point she would let me enter hers.

I had been forced to move to a less expensive area, so we lived in the same neighborhood. Ellen sometimes needed a babysitter, and we continued to meet. Ruby trusted me and apparently, Ellen did too, because a couple of times I got to spend an entire afternoon with Ruby.

Ellen still kept her distance. I felt like an unpaid babysitter that she could call on at any time, one with no life of his own or any rights. Perhaps like any babysitting grandparent.

But one day, something happened. I think it meant something. It was something so insignificant that no outsider even noticed, but to me, it was a new beginning.

Carola and her son Max were visiting. When I called her and told her about Ellen and Ruby, she booked a flight for herself and Max. During the third day of the visit, we went to a museum of photography the five of us, Carola and Max, I, Ellen and Ruby, like a big extended family. Carola and Ellen, aunt and niece, got along well.

We strolled from image to image in the airy museum, stopped, watched, discussed. Ruby got bored and fell asleep in her stroller. Carola and Ellen were both versed in the art of photography and explained the intricacies to Max and me. What you could see in the picture was not the most important thing, they both said as if they had read the same book or taken the same course. "The subtext is the most important thing," Ellen said. "The context," Carola said. We were viewing a portrait of a dancer, taken by a famous photographer. The dancer was balancing on a horse, the background was white, and there were no shadows. But the image was cropped so that you could see the lighting equipment, the roll-up background kit, and the cluttered studio. The photographer hadn't just taken a portrait of a dancer, but a photograph of the moment when the portrait was taken. Ellen explained that the intention was to create a more truthful, documentary effect by revealing the constructions behind the image. Carola added that this might not be the whole truth. Perhaps there was another layer of construction? A larger studio where this small studio was staged?

After lunch, we went to a toy store because I had promised to buy a birthday present for Ruby. When Ellen had told me about the forthcoming birthday, I didn't have the heart to tell her that it was against my faith to celebrate birthdays. At that moment, I was not a brother or a servant of truth. I was a father and a grandfather.

The shelves were filled with pink and flowery stuff, toy stoves, plush toys and dollhouses where miniature families lived. One side of each house was wide open so that anyone could see inside.

I had no idea what a girl of Ruby's age could be interested in. I asked what she would like to have.

For a moment she said nothing, she just looked at me.

"A Daddy," she said.

Ellen opened her mouth, then closed it again and stared at Ruby. Carola looked at me. Max looked at Carola. I looked at them all, one at a time.

Carola, Max, Ellen, Ruby. My flesh and blood. My family.

I bought Ruby a stuffed teddy bear.

We walked back toward the bridge and had to wait a moment for the traffic lights to change and that's when it happened. The lights switched to red for the cars, but the walking sign did not light up yet. I took a step into the street.

I felt something.

It was only a light touch.

Ellen put her hand on my arm to prevent or to warn me, probably as a reflex. I pretended not to notice her hand, but stopped. Her hand lingered for a few seconds.

Then the red light went out and the white walking man lit up and we walked across the street. It was not a remarkable moment, but that's how far she was prepared to go. It felt as if we were about to return somewhere where we had never been.

32

Throughout the spring, Ruby functioned as the lightning conductor between Ellen and me. When I suggested we spend a couple of summer weeks in Porkkala, Ellen didn't hesitate even for a moment. Carola and I had reconsidered and decided not to sell Bellevue after all.

Ellen and Ruby enjoyed the primitive cottage and the barren landscape around Bellevue. I taught them how to go in the sauna and how to fish with a spinning rod. We went out on the southernmost end of the peninsula to watch the open sea. I explained how the light from the lighthouses showed the safe route between the islands, and how in the past people sometimes lit fake fires to mislead the ships. We made a trip to Madame where Ellen's memorial still stood, though the color had eroded. One morning, we rose early and gently tiptoed up to the meadow beyond the radio mast to admire the deer that grazed in the morning dew.

Ellen was in the middle of a writing project, but she didn't want to talk about it. We arranged for her to get a few hours of writing time each day. Meanwhile, Ruby and I explored the shore, we swam, we fed the seagulls. I taught her the Bellevue rules: do not go alone to the waterfront, do not play with fire, put everything back in its proper place when you're done.

When Ellen asked me questions, I showed her pictures and old newspaper clippings we found in the attic. I told her how my little sister had played "The Gypsy Girl's Dream" on the rocky cliff. I told her about the violin competition and the get-together parties and how Ellen changed and how everyone else thought it was Mother's illness that went into her. I told her how the pain never subsided.

Ellen took notes, and I suspected that some parts of what I told her found their way into her texts.

I didn't tell her everything, I didn't even know everything myself. Perhaps I had missed the obvious. Maybe I assumed context where no context existed, maybe the dots didn't create a pattern. When a piece of the puzzle is missing, we add it in our minds. Sometimes there is a key element in a pattern that you can't spell out.

I told her about the letter Ellen left under her pillow, what she wrote about Timo. I told her how Ellen had believed that she herself was guilty and how scared she was of not being believed. I did not tell her how the light went off and how Timo drowned.

We were sitting on the terrace of the restaurant at the marina. We had had lunch and were finishing up with a cup of coffee. Ellen had completed a section of her writing and had wanted to get out, to eat at the restaurant. Ruby talked constantly. Her face was messy with ice cream and chocolate sauce. Suddenly she stopped talking mid-sentence. Without a word, she slid down from the chair and tripped off to a neighboring table. The ice cream melted in her steel cup.

A couple of children of Ruby's age had emptied a box of Lego bricks on the floor and were now building a tower.

Ruby was a fearless and confident girl. She wasn't shy with other children and frequently chatted them up. Now, she grabbed a couple of bricks and explained in English that they could build an entire city around the tower. The other children looked confused at first, and then said something in Swedish. Ruby lost her train of thought and switched to French. The answer came in Finnish.

All the restaurant customers who were sitting nearby watched in amusement how the children built their tower, in spite of the language barrier. A man at the table next to me said something about my sweet little daughter. He obviously meant Ruby. I didn't bother correcting the misconception.

I watched the people sitting around us. Tanned, friendly, apparently well-to-do people on vacation. Happy families, it seemed. They probably drew their conclusions when they saw my little family and me, but of course, they didn't know anything about us. They too were not the sum of their observable characteristics; they all had their invisible backstories that I knew nothing about.

Later that afternoon, I got to read a text that Ellen had written. It was a short section from a forthcoming novel or short story. My suspicion that she wrote about me was confirmed, but she had changed names and locations and facts. In the story, the father met the daughter when she was still pregnant, and he was the one who chose the baby's name and paid the hospital bills and fixed the apartment.

"That's not how it was," I said. "That's not true."

"The truth is overrated," she said cheerfully. "The truth is an optical illusion that you can't see if you look directly at it. Fiction is making things up that are not true, but that reveal the truth."

*

There was still some time before sunset when I steered the boat out on the open sea. Ellen didn't know yet what the excursion was about and she had already learned not to ask.

We passed the fishing rocks and the lighthouse. When I estimated that we were far enough out on the sea, I shut the engine off.

There we were, in a small boat in the middle of the sea, father and daughter, little Ruby in my arms. In the distance, we could see a white ship on its way to Tallinn or Stockholm. When the ship disappeared, it felt as if we were alone on the vast open sea.

I told Ellen and Ruby how we once had made a similar trip. I told them about the green light we never saw. I told them about the star constellations, about Cepheus and Cassiopeia, about how the North Star always stayed fixed in the north.

Ruby fell asleep in my arms. She hugged her teddy bear against her life jacket, her mouth was open, and she breathed peacefully, serene as only a sleeping child can be.

I met Ellen's gaze, she looked at Ruby and back at me and she nodded slowly and laughed, a liberated and subdued laughter, as if she finally got the punch line of a story she had heard many years before.

We probably wouldn't see any green light. Maybe we'd simply sit quietly until the sun had gone down and the stars were shining. We would talk in low voices so as not to wake Ruby up. Then we would head back into the darkening night.

We were so far from the mainland that we could only see a few fixed points. But I wasn't worried. I knew the bearings and the directions, these were well-known waters, I needed no chart, compass, or lighthouse. I remembered where the underwater rocks were and I knew the safe route home.

###

Afterword

This story is a work of fiction. The people and events are made up. Many of the geographic places do exist, but some of them I have moved from their actual locations.

The Watchtower Society served as the model for the American religious organization and its leadership and beliefs that I describe. Positions on homosexuality, on the status of women, and how women themselves may be considered guilty when they are raped, are based on information in *The Watchtower* magazine. When I described the events on Joralemon Street, I let my imagination run loose, but as background there is an article in *The Watchtower*, describing how some prominent leaders in the organization have succumbed to immoral practices like homosexuality, wife-swapping, and child molesting. I have based my descriptions of the leadership and the workings of the Governing Body on autobiographies written by former employees at the headquarters.

Current and former Jehovah's Witnesses have helped me. A special thank you goes to the unknown brother at the headquarters in New York who explained to me the procedures of the Writing Department, and to the

Coordinator of the Finnish Branch Office who helped me get some specifics right.

I have taken liberties with the chronology. For example, the express method used to build Kingdom Halls was introduced ten years later than what I describe in the novel, and the Revelation book wasn't even published at the time that Markus and Ellen examined it. A careful reader may notice that the theme of Bach's "Chaconne" does not consist of four bars, but of 4 + 4 bars. There are other places where my fiction overrides objective facts.

And finally, thank you Mary Harris, for helping me polish the English edition.

Soundtrack

Page 35: Michael Balfe, "The Gypsy Girl's Dream" from the opera *The Bohemian Girl*, 1843. Libretto by Alfred Bunn. Some readers may be familiar with Enya's version, "Marble Halls" from the album *Shepherd Moons*, 1991.

Page 35: Jean Sibelius, Violin Concerto in D Minor, Op. 47, 1905

Page 41: W. A. Mozart, "Turkish March" from Piano Sonata no.11 in A Major, K. 331, part 3, 1783

Page 53: Felix Mendelssohn, Violin Concerto in E Minor Op. 64, 2nd mvt., andante, 1844

Page 53: Vittorio Monti, *Csárdás* in D Minor, 1904

Page 54: W. A. Mozart, Violin Sonata in E Minor K. 304, 1778

Page 56: "Forward, You Witnesses!" no. 11 from *Singing and Accompanying Yourselves with Music in Your Hearts* 1966

Page 92: Niccolò Paganini, Caprice 24 in A Major, Op. 1, 1817

Page 92: Nikolai Rimsky-Korsakov, *Flight of the Bumblebee*, 1900

Page 93: J. S. Bach, *Goldberg Variations*, BWV 988, 1741, played by Glenn Gould, 1955

Page 121: Django Reinhardt, Stéphane Grappelli, "Night and Day"

Page 123: Joseph Kosma, "Autumn Leaves," 1945

Page 124: Franz Schubert, "Ave Maria," Op. 52 no. 6, 1825

Page 147: Christian Sinding, *Frühlingsrauschen*, Op. 32 no. 3, 1896

Page 147: Pablo de Sarasate, *Carmen Fantasy* for violin, Op.25, 1882

Page 175: Theo Mackeben, "Warum?" from the film *Der Student von Prag*, 1935, sung by Miliza Korjus

Page 175: Jacques Brel, "Ne me quitte pas," 1959

Page 176: Dusty Springfield, "Son of a Preacher Man," 1968, written by John Hurley and Ronnie Wilkins

Page 176: Leoš Janáček, Violin Sonata, 1914

Page 176: Henryk Wieniawski, *Fantaisie brillante sur Faust*, Op. 20, 1865

Page 176: Hurriganes, "Get On" from the album *Roadrunner*, 1974

Page 176: Linda Ronstadt, "When Will I Be Loved" from the album *Heart Like a Wheel*, 1974, written by Phil Everly

Page 180: Niccolò Paganini, Violin Sonata in E Minor, Op. 3, 1809

Page 180: Antonio Vivaldi, Violin Concerto in A Minor, Op. 3 no. 6, RV356, 1711

Page 181: Jules Massenet, "Méditation" in D Major, from the opera *Thaïs*, 1894

Page 182: J. S. Bach, "Chaconne" from Partita no. 2 for solo violin, in D Minor, BWV 1004, 1720

Page 210: Max Bruch, Violin Concerto no. 1, in G Minor, Op. 26, 1866

Page 211: Béla Bartók, Violin Concerto no. 2, BB 117, 1937–38

Page 227: Einojuhani Rautavaara, *Variétude*, Op. 82, 1974. The compulsory contemporary piece in the Sibelius Violin Competition

Page 255: Nirvana, "Rape Me" from the album *In Utero*, 1993, written by Kurt Cobain

ABOUT THE AUTHOR

Ben Kalland (b. 1959) lives in Helsinki, Finland. He writes in English, Finnish, and Swedish. His novel Vildfalken (Wild Falcon) was featured on the IBBY Honour list in 2006, and in 2018 his novel Ellen's Song was shortlisted for the Tiiliskivi Award.